THE
TRAP

Bristol Libraries

D0413378

Also by Alan Gibbons
An Act of Love
Blood Pressure
Caught in the Crossfire
The Dark Beneath
The Defender
The Edge
End Game
Hate
Julie and Me and Michael Owen Makes Three
Raining Fire

The Legendeer Trilogy

Shadow of the Minotaur
Vampyr Legion
Warriors of the Raven

The Lost Souls

Rise of the Blood Moon
Setting of a Cruel Sun

Hell's Underground

1. Scared to Death
2. The Demon Assassin
3. Renegade
4. Witch Breed

ALAN GIBBONS

THE TRAP

Orion
Children's Books

Orion Children's Books

First published in Great Britain in 2016 by Hodder and Stoughton

1 3 5 7 9 10 8 6 4 2

Text copyright © Alan Gibbons 2016

The moral rights of the author and illustrator have been asserted.

*All characters and events in this publication, other than those clearly
in the public domain, are fictitious and any resemblance to
real persons, living or dead, is purely coincidental.*

All rights reserved.

No part of this publication may be reproduced, stored in
a retrieval system, or transmitted, in any form or by any means, without
the prior permission in writing of the publisher, nor be otherwise circulated
in any form of binding or cover other than that in which it is published
and without a similar condition including this condition being
imposed on the subsequent purchaser.

A CIP catalogue record for this book
is available from the British Library.

ISBN: 978 1 78062 244 6

Typeset by Input Data Services Ltd, Bridgwater, Somerset

Printed and bound in Great Britain by CPI Group (UK) Ltd, Croydon, CR0 4YY

The paper and board used in this book are
made from wood from responsible sources.

MIX
Paper from
responsible sources
FSC® C104740
www.fsc.org

Indigo
An imprint of
Hachette Children's Group
Part of Hodder and Stoughton
Carmelite House
50 Victoria Embankment
London EC4Y 0DZ

An Hachette UK Company

www.hachette.co.uk

To all victims of terror everywhere

THE PAST

SUMMER, 2014

There were three of them, squatting uneasily on the stone-littered, reddish-brown soil while the sun blazed down. There was no mercy in the heat of the Syrian afternoon. Sweat beaded the faces of the prisoners, who had their heads bowed, hands bound behind their backs. Dark emerald cypress trees stood to attention like servile guards flanking the figure of a young gunman. He was tall and lean, his oversized combat jacket hanging loosely on his slight frame.

'Well, Majid,' his commander chuckled, 'what do we do with these three? Any thoughts?'

Majid stared blankly at the man everybody knew as Omar. He was short and wiry with shaggy, black hair and a thick, untrimmed beard. There was a hidden meaning prowling behind his words.

'You look confused, Majid. Have you forgotten what they are doing here? Look at them. They bore arms against us.'

Omar kicked at their abandoned weapons and Majid instinctively raised his XM15 semi-automatic rifle to his chest, as if presenting it for inspection. What was he meant to do? Omar was still trying to prise the correct response out of his young comrade.

'In taking sides against the mujahideen of the Islamic

1

State, they have declared themselves apostates. They are false Muslims. Don't you agree, Majid?'

For just a moment, Majid's gaze strayed to his left as he examined the faces of his fellow fighters. They were outwardly impassive, but he could read the raw fright in their eyes. He had fought alongside the captured men. He saw them as comrades in a common struggle.

'Did they not turn their weapons on us, Majid?'

Majid remembered the sudden firefight as a messy dispute about territory, an outbreak of hostilities with no clear cause, no obvious right or wrong. He had been hoping it would be easily resolved. What was the point of brothers' blood being shed in anger? One of Omar's most trusted fighters was leaning against a lone chinaberry tree, recording the scene with a hand-held camcorder. Now Majid got it. This was a test. He nodded briefly.

'Did they not kill two of your comrades?'

The answer was yes. Their bodies lay barely twenty metres away, crumpled on the parched earth, eyes staring up at the sky.

'Then you know what to do.'

Majid mustered a protest. 'I came here to heal, not to kill my brothers.'

'Only God can truly heal, Majid. If you want to save lives, you must do what is necessary.'

A man at the back of the group murmured something inaudible. Omar turned. His finger stroked the trigger of his automatic weapon.

'Something to say?'

There was no reply. Only a fool would argue with Omar. He stared at the watching fighters, eyes alive with pent-up rage. Everybody knew Omar was pressing Majid's buttons, trying to get a reaction, but they didn't know why. The scene was still being recorded. Omar turned his attention back to Majid.

2

'Is there a problem?'

By way of reply, Majid pressed the muzzle of his rifle against the back of the first captive's head.

'No problem.'

He knew that to refuse Omar was to die. Majid struggled to keep his grip firm. His hand was shaking. His mind screamed, but he dared not put his thoughts into words. Majid's finger was still lingering over the trigger when something attracted his attention, a silvery grey dart in the flawless, azure sky. The roar of an engine alerted the men to one of the regime's MiG-29 jet fighters.

The first of the aircraft's rockets was on its way before anyone could move. Flame flickered in the trail of dark smoke. There was the chatter of small arms fire and cries of 'Allahu Akbar' then the world exploded in smoke and fire. Like a tidal wave, a blast of raw energy swept over the landscape. An ear-splitting thunderclap announced a direct hit on the fighters' exposed position. The camera recording the scene continued to run.

When the smoke cleared not one man was left standing.

THE PRESENT

WEDNESDAY, 29TH JUNE

Amir is alone. He has got used to his own company. After all, what is the alternative? This is what his dad means by a new start, life without his friends. He has lived in a bubble of resentment for over a year now, as the family moved from flat to dingy flat. A crow distracts him, flapping clumsily over the yard then vanishing over the rooftops. He notices the boy in the black hoodie, sagging against the chain-link fencing. They are in the same set for English and Maths.

What are you looking at? Amir wonders. *Do you know something?*

Nikel has been watching Amir for some time. He wants to come over, but he is shy. His school uniform is dry-cleaned, his tie neatly knotted. Most of the kids have theirs pulled loose in protest at the school's latest attempt to impose a dress code. Yes, Nikel's a good boy, follows the rules, obeys his parents. Amir's dad would approve.

'Do you want something?'

Nikel looks startled.

'Well, do you?'

Nikel shrugs and comes over, takes a seat on the bench next to Amir and turns to look at him.

'You've been here a couple of months.'

Amir pulls a face. 'Observant, aren't you?'

'But you don't join in. You keep yourself to yourself.'

It's Amir's turn to stare.

'Right. I like my own company.'

'No, I don't think that's it.'

Amir's brow crumples. 'What's with you? Since when do you decide what I do or don't think?'

Nikel stands with his hands in his pockets. 'I've been watching you.'

Nikel's calm response wrong-foots Amir.

'Are you some kind of amateur detective? I told you, I keep myself to myself.'

By now, there's the hint of a smile playing around Nikel's mouth, as if he can read minds.

'I've seen you watching the other kids. You're the sociable type, but all this time you've been on the edge of things. Your sister's making friends. No, something is holding you back. Am I warm?'

The crow is back. Amir avoids Nikel's gaze.

'You don't know a thing about me.'

'Right,' Nikel answers. 'I don't, but you're not used to being a loner, I can tell that much.'

'How do you come to that conclusion, Sherlock?'

'Because I *am* a loner. I recognise the type, and you're not it.'

Amir leans back and considers Nikel.

'You're weird, you know that?'

Nikel chuckles. 'So people say.' He flicks a glance across the yard to a group of girls. Two of them are wearing hijab. A third is white, with strawberry blonde hair whipping in the wind.

'So you're twins, right, you and Nasima?'

He is nodding in the direction of the tallest girl.

'That's right, Nas is fifteen minutes older than me. She thinks she is ten years wiser.' Amir folds his arms in a show of mock suspicion. 'Fancy her, do you?'

'What if I did?'

'Oh, I'd have to kick the crap out of you. You're not Muslim.'

'How do you know that?'

'Just do.' He makes a series of passes with his hands. 'We have a secret sign, like the Freemasons.'

Nikel watches Amir's expression then laughs and punches his arm.

'That's a wind-up. You invented it.'

Amir grins.

'Had you going for a minute though, didn't I? I'd still kick your head in if you made a move on my sister.'

'Because I'm not Muslim?'

'Nah, because you're a freak of nature, geek boy.' Amir considers Nikel. 'So what's your background? Indian?'

'British.'

'Yeah, yeah, we're all British. You know what I'm asking. What about your parents?'

'British.'

'Oh, come on, give me a break. What's your . . .' Inverted-comma fingers. '. . . heritage?'

Nikel gives in.

'My grandparents came from India. Goa.'

'So you're Hindu – elephant-headed gods and all that?'

'Catholic.'

'No way! In India?'

There's a gust of wind and Nikel zips up his jacket.

'Yes, it's a Portuguese thing. They settled, generations back, and brought their religion with them.'

'I thought Goa was hippies and beach barbecues. People with bells round their necks, dancing barefoot on the sand.'

'It's got that reputation.'

Amir can see that Nikel is plucking up the courage to ask another question.

'Go on, spit it out. What's on your mind?'

'How come you moved at this time of year? I mean, it's a bit close to exams to start a new school.'

Amir has told the truth once before. It meant the family had to move on, in search of anonymity.

'Were you born nosy?' Amir asks, surprised that he doesn't feel angrier about the way Nikel is interrogating him.

'Probably. So what's the answer?'

Amir laughs.

'You're not getting one.'

Because answers mean danger.

Nikel considers his refusal.

'Fair enough.' Then, without so much as a pause, he moves on. 'Heard about what happened to that newsagent round the corner?'

Amir doesn't respond. Nikel ploughs on regardless.

'England Awakes kicked his head in the other night.'

'How do you know it was them?'

'They were shouting while they were beating him.' Nikel is watching Amir's expression. 'So, England Awakes: you've heard of it?'

Amir sees angry men, Union flags, the cross of St George. 'I don't live on Mars. Too right wing for the EDL. Too ugly for TV. This newsagent: how badly was he hurt?'

'Broken ribs. Fractured wrist. I smell trouble. There's a march at the weekend. Saturday. They've been spraying slogans on walls. *Torch the mosque*, that sort of thing.' He expects an answer. There isn't one. 'Anyway, the streets are going to be in lock-down. The council says the mosque can expand. England Awakes has got a campaign against it: Dump the Dome.'

Amir refuses to be drawn.

'Catchy.'

'Don't you care? They put the guy in hospital.'

'Seriously, what's it got to do with me?'

'You're Muslim. They're targeting your mosque. I thought you'd be raging.'

The bell rings to announce the end of lunchtime. Amir gets to his feet. 'Who cares, so long as they leave me alone?'

At that moment three boys jostle their way through the crush. Nikel watches them then drops his eyes when they turn his way. Amir registers the group.

'I'm guessing they're not fans of multiculturalism.'

Nikel rolls his eyes, lets the group pass and sets off towards the main building.

'Got it in one. A piece of advice: steer well clear.'

2

Kate Armstrong decides to save half her Pret sandwich for later, puts the cardboard and cellophane wrapper in her bag and crosses Horseferry Road towards the Grade II listed building where she works. The monolith that houses MI5 stands on the north bank of the Thames, overlooking Lambeth Bridge. Kate is jittery. Competent as her superiors believe she is, Kate is prone to anxiety, even self-doubt. Maybe that's what makes her so effective. She lives in a permanent state of tension. The devil, she knows, is in the detail, and Kate Armstrong is very good at detail.

She is an experienced recruiter and handler of agents. She didn't think anything about the job could surprise her, but that was before a new arrival appeared on the scene, codename Bungee, in south-eastern Turkey. He was a bewildered young man with multiple, untreated injuries and a haunted look in his eyes.

She remembers the call from Six and instinctively glances across the Thames in the direction of the SIS building. The phone call from MI6 didn't come from the odd, ziggurat-shaped monolith at Vauxhall Cross, but from its station in Turkey. The voice on the line belonged to Hugh Aspinall, a rising star in the security services. She had met him on a number of occasions and trusted his judgement. His opening gambit was enticing.

'I might have something for you, Kate.'

'Let me guess, you've bought me a box of baklava.'

'Oh, this is tastier than baklava.'

'OK,' Kate told him, 'you've dangled the bait quite long enough, thank you very much. I'm hooked. What have you got?'

'It's a bit of an oddity really. We took a phone call last week from the Austrian consulate in Gaziantep.'

What is this, she thought, The Sound of Music? Austria wasn't the kind of place that came up on the radar of the security forces very often. She suppressed the urge to crack a joke about yodelling.

'Gaziantep? I'm not familiar with the name.'

'It's near the Syrian border. It's starting to get a reputation as a jihadi crossing point.'

The mention of Syria had Kate leaning forward, propping her elbows on her desk. The civil war in Syria and the spread of Islamic State insurgency through neighbouring Iraq had made the region a hotspot for international terrorism. Anticipating what Hugh was going to tell her, she had a stab at spelling it out.

'Are you telling me one of our black-garbed friends wants out?'

'I'm telling you that a twenty-year-old male from London by the name of Majid Sarwar recently stumbled into the Austrian consulate, much the worse for wear, and asked where he could find the nearest British Embassy.'

'Worse for wear?'

'As in: how the hell are you still breathing?'

'So what did you do?'

'After discussions with the Embassy staff, we arranged for a car to pick him up. He was badly hurt. I'll send through some pictures. The right side of his face is a mess, half-melted by ordnance. God knows how he got as far as he did in that condition. If there is one thing we know about him, he is as tough as proverbial old boots.'

'Or he has a lust for life.'

'Yes, that too.'

'He's still just another jihadi fighter having second thoughts.'

'Not quite. Our boy was a medical student before he took the trip to the Turkish border. He is intelligent and well-connected.'

Kate processed that last word. Well-connected?

'And where is he now?'

'We're taking good care of him. He is receiving first-class medical attention. We've got him in a private ward and he is under twenty-four-hour guard. There is talk of plastic surgery.'

'Reformed jihadi health insurance?'

'He isn't reformed yet, but we're working on it.'

'Fine,' she said, 'I'm with you so far, but what's so special about this particular absconder? Young men and women have gone to Syria before, thinking they are defending their oppressed brothers and sisters from Assad's war machine.'

She went on, 'You've heard the Home Secretary's recent statement. Your guy chose to come out to a war zone. No excuses, no ifs or buts, these people have a good idea what they're getting into when they go. The government is taking a hard line. So you've got a jihadi who realises he's made a mistake. He's a big boy. Let him explain his circumstances to a court of law.'

Hugh heard her out. If a silence could be smug, that's how Kate would have described the next few seconds.

'OK, Hugh, I know you've got something else. Stop holding out on me.'

'What if this guy is different?' Hugh said. 'And what if he name-dropped Bashir Mirza?'

The instant Kate heard the name, the back of her neck prickled. Bashir's activities had set off all kinds of alarms before he went missing several months earlier.

'And what,' Hugh concluded with a flourish, 'if the name David Obi, aka Abu Rashid, also came up in conversations?'

By then Kate was salivating. Bashir and Abu Rashid continued to rumble ominously on the radar. They had come up *in a briefing only a week earlier. If the absconder knew how to get to them, he could be a vital asset.*

'In that case,' she said, 'I would be very interested. I might even put in a request for a business class ticket to Istanbul.'

'So you would like to work together on this project?' Hugh asked.

'It's a distinct possibility,' Kate answered.

She remembers everything about that fateful phone call: the muddy light in her office, the drone of the traffic, the wail of the police siren in the distance. 7 July, 2005 was over a decade ago, but the wound was fresh. Kate had been new to the job then. She had been on leave and was driving back to London when the overhead signs lit up all along the motorway. The message is imprinted on her: AVOID LONDON. AREA CLOSED.

That summer's morning, fifty-two innocent people were killed and seven hundred were injured. The thought of a repeat attack haunted Kate and every one of her colleagues. A motto was established. *We have to get lucky every time. The terrorists only have to get lucky once.*

She returns to her desk, remembers her sandwich and starts to eat. She chews thoughtfully and picks up the framed photograph of her husband and daughters. She finds herself smiling, remembering the way they burst through the door and leapt on the bed that morning. Then an image fills her mind: a fire flash, spraying glass, a roiling mass of flame and smoke. She imagines her family's faces curling and blackening, then being blown away like ash. It takes something big to keep Kate awake at night, but this image is one of them.

In a few minutes she will put a call through to her immediate superior, Jennifer Sherbourne. It is over a year since Majid Sarwar came into her life. He has come good with his promise to contact Bashir Mirza.

Now it is time to activate him.

3

It is nine miles as the crow flies from Thames House to the cramped, rented flat above a Turkish restaurant in north London where Amir Sarwar lives with his twin sister and their parents. From Thames House, the view is of London's history, power and majesty. It is just two miles to the Houses of Parliament, another half a mile past that to Buckingham Palace. Every way you turn there are echoes of the past. In contrast, the streets around the flat are a jumble. Here, people concentrate on making ends meet. A forty-five-minute drive from Kate Armstrong's office overlooking the river, Nasima is beating her twin brother up the stairs.

'Loser!' she teases, as she turns her key in the lock.

'You are really sad,' Amir sighs, tossing his bag on the sofa.

Nasima wishes Amir wasn't so subdued. He has been this way for months and he doesn't show any sign of snapping out of it. She doesn't say anything. She has had to get used to his moods. Once upon a time, it was three of them jostling through the door after a sprint along the street. Majid and Amir were thick as thieves back then. Nasima hears their voices as if Majid were still here.

'I gave you a twenty-metre start and I still beat you home.' *Majid boasted.*

'You wait until I'm your age,' Amir yelled.

Majid, wrapped his arm round his younger brother's neck.
'You'll never be my age, you idiot.'
Amir, squirmed in the headlock: 'You know what I mean.'
Nasima's eyes sting as she remembers.

'We're home,' she calls, knowing Majid will never be home again. A hand of darkness took him.

'Do you really think I didn't hear you coming?' her mum answers. 'You thunder up those stairs like a pair of baby elephants.'

Amir peers round the kitchen door where she is browning chicken in onion, ginger and garlic paste.

'It isn't our fault. There's no carpet on those stairs. I thought Dad was supposed to bring it up with the landlord. How long are we going to be in this dump anyway?'

'Once we have a buyer for our house, we will start looking for somewhere. This is only short-term. We won't be here forever, Amir.'

'That's what you said in the last flat and the one before that. When do we get to settle down? It's a year since we had a normal life.'

Mum sighs.

'Why do we have to have this discussion over and over again? When your brother shamed us, we had no choice but to look for somewhere else to live.'

'You're the one who had to open his mouth and tell somebody who we were,' Nasima reminds him. 'That's why we had to move the last time.'

Amir scowls.

'That's right, blame me.'

'I'm not blaming you,' Nasima says. 'I'm just saying there's a reason for all the moves.'

'We could have kept our heads up,' Amir protests, 'and stayed where we were. The only reason we're doing this is Dad's pride.'

Amir growls his frustration. 'Majid, Majid, Majid. That's all I ever hear. When are you going to accept that he's dead and gone?'

'Amir, that's enough!'

He sees his mum's chin tremble and rushes an apology.

'I'm sorry, Ammi-ji. I didn't mean it. You know I didn't mean it. That was thoughtless.' His arms flop at his sides. He didn't want to hurt her. He wanted . . . he wanted what was no longer possible. 'I'm just fed up of living like this.'

Nasima fumbles in her sleeve for a tissue.

'It's OK, Nasima. It's just the mention of his name. I know it's stupid, but I still expect him to come walking through the door.'

Nasima flashes a warning at Amir. *Don't do that again.*

'Don't cry, Ammi-ji. Please.'

'I'm fine.' She laughs. 'Out of my kitchen, you two. You're going to make me burn the garlic.'

Nasima pushes Amir roughly as they leave the kitchen.

'What's wrong with you?' she hisses.

'I didn't think.'

Everybody says Nasima has a placid nature, but she can be fiery in defence of her mother.

'That's your problem. You never do. You're just like . . .'

Amir shakes his head, anticipating the end of her sentence.

'Is that right? I'm just like Majid? I loved my brother, Nasima, but no way am I like him. Tell me, when did I run off to Syria and pick up an AK-47? When did I start talking about the khalifa?'

Nasima tilts her head. 'I think it's my turn to say sorry.' She sees his bag on the sofa. 'If you want a quiet life, you need to move that before Dad gets home.'

Amir takes a deep breath, decides against arguing, and marches into his room. He kicks the door shut behind him and shoves his bag under the bed. He glances out of the window at the tiny yard below. Greyish mist cloaks the streets. There's a knock at the door. Amir is unable to quell the smile that springs to his lips. That will be Nasima come to make up. She hates conflict. He is glad she always makes the first move.

'Yes?'

'It's me. Can I come in?'

Amir opens the door to let her in. She holds out a flat, upturned palm.

'Peace?'

Amir grins and brings his hand down on hers in a playful slap.

'Peace. Sorry. I just want to go home.'

'You and me both.'

'Is it too much to want our old lives back? I don't understand.'

Nasima feels sorry for her brother. While she is just about able to accept her lot, Amir craves his mates, his old routines. She has already made new friends, but he prowls around on his own, brooding about the past.

'It isn't going to happen, is it? You know what Dad says.'

That sets Amir off. Soon, he mimics his dad's deep, fractious voice.

I can't hold my head up in the street. Majid brought shame to this family. I can't walk down to the shops without somebody staring at me, thinking I am a bad father. No, I will not stay in this house another day: not one more day.

Nasima smiles.

'You've got him down to a tee.' Then a chuckle. 'Just don't do it when he's around.'

Raindrops rap on the window. Amir flops on the bed and stares up at the ceiling. He follows the pattern of a large crack. There are two brown circles where water has come through in the past.

Three lousy flats.

Three rain-damaged ceilings.

'No chance of that. I'd never hear the end of it.' He continues the impression. '*Where is your respect? Do you think I work all the hours God sends to have you acting like a clown?*' He loves the way Nasima laughs at his impression and lays it on even more thickly for her benefit. '*You are going to grow big clown feet and a big clown nose to go with your big clown head.*'

Before long the pair of them are doubling up with laughter, voices echoing around the flat. Just then, the door goes.

'Shush. That's Dad coming in now.'

They spill out of the room and stand to mock attention. Laughter is still bubbling on their lips. Nasima's eyes are sparkling.

'Welcome home, Abbu-ji.'

Amir follows her lead.

'Yes, welcome home, Abbu-ji.'

Their father frowns.

'What's got into you two?'

Mum appears.

'I think they've been at the laughing gas.'

Dad pulls the *Evening Standard* from under his arm. He turns three pages, laying it out on the table.

'Have you seen this?'

They gather round and read the headline.

Councillors say: mosque marchers not welcome.

'Sometimes it feels as if trouble follows this family around. We don't seem to be able to cut a break.'

Nasima picks up the newspaper and skim-reads the article.

'What do these England Awakes people mean, no new mosque? There's a mosque on the site already. All they are doing is extending the building.'

She remembers seeing the plans for a new study centre.

'These are not rational people, Nasima. They are intent on causing trouble.'

Nasima throws the paper down in disgust, but it is Amir who comments.

'They're dangerous idiots. Some of the kids at school are going down there on Saturday. They're planning a welcoming party.'

Nasima stares.

'You knew about this already? You didn't say anything to me.'

'Nikel only told me about it today.'

'Nikel? What, the dorky one in your Maths set? Hair like a Mr Whippy ice cream?'

'That's him.'

'Does that mean His Royal Majesty Amir has finally decided to make friends with the locals?'

Their father cuts in.

'You listen to me, both of you. You will not go near the mosque on Saturday. You will not go within a mile of it.'

That's a novelty, Nasima thinks, *telling them* not *to go to the mosque.*

'Do you hear me?'

Amir can't help himself.

'Dad, the whole street can hear you.'

At that, his father's head snaps round. Amir drops his eyes instantly.

'Sorry, Abbu-ji.'

He feels his hand on his shoulder, squeezing.

'You will not make a joke out of this, Amir. Do you really not understand what I am saying? I have lost one son. I will not lose another.'

Amir is close to tears.

'Dad,' Nasima says, 'you're not going to lose him. Amir is a good boy, a sensible boy. He works hard at school.'

She can see her father's fingers burying themselves into Amir's shoulder. His voice is low.

'Majid was a bright boy too. He could have been a doctor, a solicitor, a well-paid professional.' He takes a breath. 'Instead, he chose to go running into the arms of those fanatics, those takfiri zealots. It is not just intelligence that matters, Amir. It is common sense. You get these big ideas when you are young and you start chasing all kinds of crazy dreams. You have to stay grounded, both of you.' His attention is all on Amir. 'Do you understand me?'

'Yes, Abbu-ji.'

'Nasima?'

She wants to ask what she has done to make him ask such a question, but she keeps her thoughts to herself.

'Yes, Abbu-ji. Of course.'

As Nasima goes into her room she, like Amir, has something at the back of her mind.

It spells danger.

THE PAST

AUTUMN, 2014

Nasima was home alone when she saw Dad's car thumping on to the drive. The headlights swept through the windows. Nasima never drew the curtains when she was doing her homework. She liked to look out at the night. Hearing Dad kill the engine, she left her books on the bed and jogged downstairs.

To her surprise, as she went to open the door, she saw that Dad was talking to somebody. It was a few moments before she recognised him: Majid's friend, Bashir. Her heart kicked. He was the reason Majid walked out of the house. He was the reason . . . for everything. Throat tight with anxiety, Nasima opened the door. Bashir was wagging his finger in Dad's face.

'This is the only warning I will give you, old man. If the police come calling, and you breathe a word about me, I will come back.' His eyes glittered. 'I will come for you.'

He reached for something in his jacket pocket. Nasima saw the flash of a blade.

'You've got a lot to lose, Naveed: your wife, your second son, your obedient daughter.'

Dad's eyes were wild.

'Come near my family and I will—'

Bashir leaned forward.

'Yes? What will you do? Come after me with your baseball

bat? That went well last time.' He smirked. 'You're out of your league.'

The words were no sooner out of his mouth than Bashir glimpsed Nasima watching. He nodded in her direction.

'Remember what I said. You have a lot to lose.'

Dad watched Bashir walking away down the street and glanced at Nasima.

'How much of that did you hear?'

'I heard enough. Dad, do you really think he would hurt us?'

Dad nodded.

'I wouldn't put anything past somebody like him.' His gaze ran down the hall. 'Are they still out?'

Nasima nodded.

'Listen. I am going to ask you a very big favour, Nasima. Please keep quiet about this. Don't say a word to either of them. I don't want them worrying.'

'Yes, Abbu-ji.'

Bashir had gone, but Nasima could still feel his presence like a cruel wind brushing against her cheek.

THE PRESENT

4

WEDNESDAY, 29TH JUNE

The mood in the family home would be very different if they knew Majid was alive. Kate Armstrong's agent, codenamed Bungee, has just boarded the train from Cambridge to Kings Cross. He thinks about his handler. He only has one way to contact her: the SIM card storing her number that he has sewn into the waistband of his jeans. He finds an unreserved seat opposite a couple in their fifties.

'May I borrow your newspaper?' he asks.

'Help yourself.'

Majid registers the wife's brooding gaze, the undercurrent of hostility. He has seen this kind of look before. He will see it again. Majid closes his eyes and remembers three kids looking for answers, but all he found on that tract of parched earth on the Syrian-Turkish border was death. Now he is on his way back to London, where his journey started. Kate has promised that an A4 surveillance team will be there when he leaves the train. They will watch his every step, follow his every move. He remembers his pact with Kate. *A Devil's pact*, Bashir would say, *selling your soul to the Kuffar*.

He remembers Kate's words. 'Be careful. You will be in danger – there is no avoiding that – but you will be protected every step of the way. Believe me, we know our business. We will do everything to keep you safe. In return, you will obtain the information we need to prevent an atrocity.'

That's the deal. He is a prized asset, a man who matters. Leaning his forehead against the window, he watches the countryside flash by. He feels tired. It has been this way for weeks. It is as if the decision he has taken weighs him down like a great rock. It is one thing to walk away from the horror of the Syrian conflict. It is another to serve the British state. He looks at the front page of the newspaper:

Threat Level Critical.

And the strap line:

Home Secretary advises vigilance. A terrorist attack could be imminent.

The man opposite catches his eye then nudges his wife and leads her to empty seats just down the carriage. Majid is half out of his seat, tempted to go after the couple and confront them, when he notices somebody watching. An Asian guy down the aisle is paying close attention. To Majid's surprise, he comes over.

'Salaam alaikum.'

After a moment's hesitation, Majid replies.

'Wa alaikum assalaam.'

The newcomer follows Majid's gaze to where the couple are sitting.

'They're not worth it.' There is an offered hand. 'I'm Nabil.'

Majid takes the hand in a firm grip. That kid on the street corner is a dead man. He is dead to his family and to everyone who knew him: almost two years dead. He has a different identity now, codename Bungee, and a name for moments such as this.

'Usman.'

'Nice to meet you.'

Majid examines the man's jacket and the crisp, white shirt beneath, the smartly pressed trousers, the designer glasses.

'What do you do for a living, Nabil?'

'I'm a lawyer.'

Majid nods.

'You've got a piece of wisdom to impart, yeah?'

'Don't let them provoke you.'

'So that's it, you're meant to carry on regardless? Keep calm and say salaam?'

Nabil checks the messages on his phone.

'We make a life. We make a good life.'

The train is pulling into Hitchin. Nabil gets to his feet.

'This is my stop.'

'Not carrying on to London?'

'No. I'm guessing you are. You sound like a Londoner, Usman.'

'Yes, you tagged me right.'

'So what's waiting for you when you get to London? Family, friends?'

Majid looks straight ahead. Once upon a time he had all that: family, friends, a future. Now he has a mission.

'Come on, sum it up in one word. What do you expect to find?'

Majid shrugs. 'Closure.'

'Closure?'

'Yes. I've had things happen in my life. I need to get them sorted. Closure.'

Nabil picks up his phone.

'I hope you find it.'

'Me too,' Majid murmurs.

He doesn't notice Nabil melt into the crowd on the platform and board the next carriage down. He is lost in thought, drawn to the past.

THE PAST

AUTUMN, 2013

There was a huddle of young men on a London street corner. They were all wearing the same uniform: baseball caps, black North Face jackets, tracksuit bottoms and trainers. All but one was sporting a keffiyeh scarf.

'Is your dad still on at you over the other night, Majid?'

A shrug. 'He thinks you guys are a dangerous influence on me.'

There was laughter.

'He's got that right.'

'All he ever talks about is the revision I have to do for my exams. Yes, like university is going to solve everything. All over the world, our brothers and sisters are dying.'

Each had an emptiness inside him, and there was nothing to fill it.

They talked about the crap they got from the police and the suspicion they encountered everywhere. They talked about harassment and insults. They talked about being British and Muslim and the way they were always seen as a threat.

'They repeated *Four Lions* last week. My dad was disgusted.' Majid put on his father's voice. 'You think this is funny? It makes Muslims look like a bunch of crazies.'

Yusuf cackled.

'That sheep, bro? Hysterical. Instant mutton.'

They started to shout lines from the movie.

'I used different voices.'

'IRA voices.'

'She's got a beard.'

Then they all had their hands over their mouths.

'I covered it.'

They fell about laughing, then they talked about school and parents and being misunderstood. They talked about exclusion and religion. They talked about the pity of war and the treatment of their brothers and sisters in far-off Syria.

'Somebody should do something. They're dropping barrel bombs on civilians. That's just evil.'

'What's a barrel bomb?'

'Explosives shoved in a barrel and dropped from a plane. Does what it says on the tin.'

Jamil turned serious.

'If you want to do something about it, I know people. I've got contacts.'

The claim was met by mocking laughter.

'You've got nothing. Go on, big man, who are your contacts?'

'I know a guy.'

'You know nothing, bro. You need a compass to cross the road.'

The three friends were idealists and their ideals swirled around a conflict two thousand miles away. These conversations belonged to a time less than two years ago, but to Majid they might as well belong to another century. It was then that decisions were taken that would change their lives in ways they could barely imagine.

Majid saw the faces of these boys in the amber glow of the streetlamp and he smiled at their names: Yusuf and Jamil. Their friendship would one day be shattered in a few seconds of shock, fire and debris. Jamil was talking.

'You can laugh, but you've got to meet Bashir. He's different.'

'Different how?'

'Exciting. I mean, he knows where he's going. He doesn't take crap from anybody. He knows the guys who matter. Different people, different vibe, a different message.'

'My dad will go nuts if you're introducing me to some Salafist group.'

'So don't tell him. You're not a kid any more. Talk to anybody you like. It's your life.'

And it was true. These three young men weren't kids. They were waiting for exam results, college and independence. Majid was planning to be a doctor, Yusuf a systems analyst. Only Jamil faced an uncertain future. But they had more on their minds than education.

'You've got to meet him.'

'Bashir doesn't ask you to be patient and wait for the white guy to accept you. He doesn't think you should be grateful because they've stopped Paki-bashing. He makes a lot of sense, not like the imam at Central.'

This struck a chord. They were bored of all the pleas for moderation.

'Him,' Yusuf grunted, 'he doesn't listen to the youth. He just likes getting his picture taken with the MPs and the Commissioner of Police.' He put on a sermon voice. '*You don't need to remind us about your Prevent strategy here. We broadcast every word we say for the whole world to hear. Islam is a religion of peace.*'

Jamil laughed and nudged Majid.

'You haven't said much.'

'Nothing to say. I'm listening.'

'I don't have the words,' Jamil said. 'You've got to meet Bashir. This guy, he's lived. He's got the scar tissue to prove it. He's done real bad stuff: crime, drugs, life on the streets.'

Majid pulled a face.

'You think that's something to be proud of?'

Jamil stumbled for a moment, then pressed on.

'Let me finish my story, yeah? He's done time. The justice system doesn't know what to do with people like Bashir, but he didn't need counsellors to find his way. He left all that behind when he became a true Muslim.'

'So what was he before?'

'He was lost, that's what he was. He was on his own.'

And that resonated. For all the joking around, they were all curious about Bashir.

'Then he returned to Allah. Wait till you meet him. He's like a magnet. There's something about him that just draws you. The way he talks! He explains everything so clearly. We can be the generation that changes everything. We can go down in history.'

THE PRESENT

THURSDAY, 30TH JUNE

The Sarwar family is finishing breakfast. The morning news is running in the background. There is an item about two men getting arrested as they returned to the UK from Syria. Mum goes to turn it off.

'No, I want to hear.'

Nasima and Amir swap glances. Dad still reacts to every mention of the war zone where their elder brother fell.

'This is the madness that took our son. We can't pretend nothing happened. I need to understand.'

Dad continues to watch, a muscle twitching in his cheek as he sets his jaw. Presently, the face of a middle-aged Asian man fills the screen. He is bearded and wears a white skullcap. A caption identifies him as Ibrahim Al-Quraishi, imam at a London mosque.

'We shouldn't go jumping to conclusions,' he is saying. 'We don't know what these people were doing there.'

The presenter presses him.

'It is hard to imagine an innocent explanation, Mr Al-Quraishi.'

'I am sure that many people have gone to Syria for humanitarian reasons. You have to remember, this crisis did not start out as the war it is now. In the beginning, there were peaceful civil rights protests.'

The presenter dismisses the explanation. 'What if their activities in Syria were related to terrorism?'

'There is no proof of that. Some of the people who travelled from the UK did so to aid people suffering from Assad's attacks. Is it not possible that when things got difficult they decided it was time to return home?'

'So we just pat them on the head and let them carry on as usual?'

'Of course not. The Danish government has a programme in place to de-radicalise people coming back. Anyone returning should be interviewed rigorously. If they have genuinely made a mistake they should be able to resume their old lives. Who better than a former fighter to warn young people of what they might face out there? Should we not all be afforded a second chance? Can you say in all honesty that you have never made a mistake?'

This seems to enrage the interviewer.

'So you're saying they're all innocents?'

Al-Quraishi is not playing the game. 'Please do not twist my words.'

'What if they oppose everything this country stands for? You do know that there have been a number of devastating jihadi plots in recent years.'

'Then those taking part should face the full force of the law.' Al-Quraishi steeples his fingers and lodges them under his chin. 'Look, if the government insists on stiff sentences for everyone coming back, regardless of what they have done, or whether they regret it, these people will just decide it is better to stay where they are and continue to be influenced by groups such as Islamic State. If we have such an inflexible attitude, how will we reintroduce people to British society? Isn't integration the aim?'

'This Al-Quraishi seems a good man,' Dad admits, 'a pragmatist. I wish Majid had trusted such a man instead of that thug Bashir. Maybe . . .' He blinks repeatedly, fighting off a tear, and walks to the door. 'I must be going. I will be late.'

'We'd better get off too,' Nasima says. 'Coming, Amir?'

'Give me a minute,' he says. 'I've got to get my bag. Some busybody told me to put it in my room.'

Mum makes eye contact with Nasima and they both smile. Sixty seconds later, Mum is alone in the flat. She takes a small, crumpled photograph from her purse and draws her thumb across the familiar features.

'Majid,' she murmurs.

THE PAST

AUTUMN, 2013

This is how it began, with a group of men on a street corner.

Majid was quiet. Yet another quarrel with his father was booming in his head. Nothing he ever did was right.

'Where are you going?'

'Why are you not studying?'

'Do you think you can become a doctor without hard work?'

Then the words that sent Majid storming into the night.

'I am ordering you not to go out.'

'Order,' Majid snorted. 'It's all you ever do.'

That was his father all over. Always shouting the odds, never listening. He was harder on Majid than either Amir or Nasima. He expected more from his elder son.

Bashir was looking straight at Majid. 'Did you say something?'

'No, I was thinking . . . out loud. Sorry.'

Bashir continued to study Majid. His gaze was fixed and unblinking.

'Your friends tell me you have been doing charity work.'

Majid dug his hands in his pockets self-consciously. It sounded like criticism.

'Yes, I want to do something to help. The Syrian regime is butchering its people.'

'Your instincts are sound, Majid, but do you really think you are going to make a difference?'

The others were intrigued.

'I hope so,' Majid said, his voice trailing off.

'You are sending blankets, tents, medicine. That is good.'

It didn't sound good. A but was on the way.

'Do you think blankets will stop tanks and planes? Are tents going to stop the massacres?'

'It will help the victims get through the winter.'

Bashir reached out a strong hand and squeezed Majid's shoulder. For a moment, Majid flinched. It reminded him of his father.

'Only God protects the weak, God and those who serve him.'

Majid flicked an awkward glance at his friends.

'You have a good heart, Majid,' Bashir continued, 'but you need to use your head. Charity is good, but it is no more than a sticking plaster. What you have to do is close the wound. There is only one way to do that for good.'

'And that is—?'

'Bring down the infidel regime,' Yusuf said, interrupting. 'Isn't that right, Bashir?'

Bashir ignored Yusuf. He was devoting all his attention to Majid.

'The mujahideen are arming themselves, my brothers. They will destroy the murder machine and establish a caliphate where all will live in peace according to sharia law, but they need recruits. All they have is combat rifles against the most advanced military hardware.' He dropped his voice. 'If you want to wipe away the tears of the women and children, you must break the butcher's power at the source. The Muslim Ummah must not let our Syrian brothers and sisters bleed to death.'

Majid watched the way his friends' eyes blazed. He didn't

know how to argue with a man like Bashir. There was such certainty in everything he said. He spoke of God's justice.

'Inform yourself, Majid.' Bashir pulled out his phone. 'Don't believe everything you see on the BBC or ITV. They are just Zionist mouthpieces. Give me your email and I will send you links to some good sites.' He took Majid's phone and typed the address into his own. 'There is already a civil war. Forget everything you have heard until this moment. Make yourself anew. I am talking about jihad, Majid. The battle lines are drawn. You are either with us or against us.'

THE PRESENT

6

THURSDAY, 30TH JUNE

'Looks like you've found yourself a new friend, Amir.'

Nasima picks out Nikel with a flick of her head. For a moment, Nikel seems excited that she has acknowledged his existence. Amir leaves Nasima with her friend Lucy.

He puts Nikel straight about his sister.

'Don't get your hopes up. She was only telling me you were waiting. There's no interest there, my friend.'

Nikel doesn't seem over-concerned. Amir guesses that he has never had much luck with girls. If you've got low expectations, you're never disappointed.

'Going to English?'

Nikel shakes his head.

'We've got a Year Ten assembly instead. Didn't you read the newsletter?'

'I make it my business never to read school newsletters. What's the assembly about?'

'It can only be two things,' Nikel tells him. 'Either it's another lecture to tell us to get our act together for our exams or —'

There is an interruption from a blond-haired boy to their left.

'It's not that. They're going to warn us off the England Awakes march.'

He sticks out a hand and Amir shakes it.

'Tomasz. With a Z at the end.'

'What's that, Polish?'

'Got it in one.'

Nikel looks put out that Tomasz has muscled in on their budding friendship.

Their conversation draws the interest of three passing boys.

'I wouldn't hang out with that lot, Tomasz. I hear it's catching.'

'What is?'

'Jihad.'

'I'll tell you what's catching, Jace: stupidity.'

Jace flips him the finger. Tomasz returns the gesture with extra venom. He gives Jace time to drift out of hearing before he says another word.

'That's England Awakes, Junior Moron Division.'

There is movement towards the hall. Amir follows the crowd. Tomasz and Nikel follow. The hall is filling up rapidly. Teachers position themselves next to their class or mess with their laptops. The supply teachers shift their feet, wondering what they're supposed to do. A shaft of watery sunlight falls on the front rows of the assembly.

Before long, the members of staff signal that the students should be quiet.

'Hey, it's Mr Lucas,' Tomasz notes. 'We are honoured. I wonder what's brought Zeus down from Mount Olympus.' He looks at Mr Lucas' companions. 'Who've we got here?'

There are three men following Mr Lucas. One is a vicar, complete with dog collar.

'They're rolling out the men of God,' Amir tells him. 'Vicar. The second guy is Sikh.'

The third man is dressed in a brown kurta and a skull cap.

'And that's the imam from the mosque.'

'The one you go to?'

36

'Yes, sometimes.'

Tomasz watches them taking their seats.

'Looks like they're covering all bases.'

Nikel grins.

'They're missing a Jedi knight.'

Mr Lucas introduces the faith leaders. One by one, they advise the students to stay well away from the area of the mosque on Saturday.

'These people are being bussed into our community to stir up trouble,' the imam says. 'We are appealing to all sections of our community to stay away from the area. We do not want outsiders dividing us.'

He is about to continue when there is a ripple of laughter two rows behind. Somebody snorts into his hand. The whole assembly turns round. Teachers dart to the spot, glaring as they seek out the culprits. Jace has got his head down. His friends' shoulders are shaking as they try to suppress laughter. The imam glances at Mr Lucas then finishes his speech.

'The best thing to do, faced with outside agitators and trouble-makers, is to ignore them. A week on Saturday, there will be a faith camp attended by all members of our community. At this event, we will be promoting peace and understanding, not confrontation. It is an eight-mile journey, but I hope some of you will be able to attend.'

Mr Lucas thanks the imam and makes his closing remarks.

'I know that some of you will have seen the leaflets from England Awakes and its opponents, or come across them on social networking. Maybe you sympathise with one or other of these groups. My advice to you is to steer clear of any trouble. Conflict will get this community nowhere. We have a proud tradition of tolerance and respect in our school. I expect it to continue. Details of the faith camp that was mentioned by Mr Aziz are in this week's school newsletter. Thank you. Teachers, you may take your classes.'

There is somebody waiting for Majid on the concourse. Bashir Mirza has his arms folded and greets him with a look of quiet amusement.

'Salaam alaikum.'

'Wa alaikum assalaam.'

Bashir unfolds his arms and embraces Majid.

'Welcome back.'

He releases Bashir and leads the way out of the station.

'This way.'

Majid looks at the hurrying crowds, the queue to get a Harry Potter photo, the clusters of people gazing up at the information boards. He wonders if this could be the target, if all these men, women and children with their everyday hopes, dreams and anxieties are in Bashir's firing line.

'Long time, no see.'

'Yes, a lot has happened.'

'The war happened. How are your injuries, Rocket Man?'

Instinctively, Majid touches the side of his face where the blast burned through his skin.

'It still keeps me awake sometimes.'

'But no lasting damage?'

Majid wonders how to answer. How do you assess damage?

He relives the MiG-29 attack every night. He hears the crack of ordnance and feels the raw, unstoppable power of the impact. He sees his comrades torn to bits, body parts blackening in the aftermath of the explosion.

Majid remembers when he believed all Bashir's lies. He swallowed every one, every over-egged story of his links with the mujahideen all over the world. He wants to say he was a kid then, but it wasn't that long ago. He knew what he was doing. Majid recognises Bashir for what he is: a dangerously unstable free agent with a grievance, a man who has gathered six, eight, ten co-conspirators to kill and maim in the name of a faith he twists for his own purposes.

Majid realises he hasn't answered Bashir's question.

'No, no lasting damage.'

They cross Euston Road with its noodle bars, coffee shops and bookmakers. Bashir pulls a fob from his pocket and unlocks the last in a row of cars. Majid makes a mental note of the number plate to pass on to Kate.

'I envy you.'

'Really? Why?'

Bashir glances at Majid as if pitying him.

'Look back there: false people living false lives. You got to fight the idol-worshippers and the hypocrites. My brother, you are a warrior of jihad.'

Majid remembers the way he lay on a bed of stones, pain tearing his flesh like a cheese grater. He remembers how he cried for his mother as his skin burned.

'I went out there to treat the wounded.'

Bashir grins.

'Save the sob story for somebody else. This is Bashir you're talking to.'

'What do you mean? I did.'

Bashir isn't impressed.

'Didn't stay that way though, did it? There isn't a man born of woman who doesn't like the feel of a rifle in his hands. Admit it. It's the excitement.'

Majid doesn't answer. They get in the car and pull away from the kerb.

'Where are we going?'

'Safe house.'

'How safe?'

Bashir slaps Majid's leg.

'I like your style, Rocket Man. You always had a sense of humour.'

I must have done, Majid thinks. Once he saw a revolutionary, a man who could inspire. Now he sees a thug, a bully, a fake.

'Five have got eyes on us, man, but we've got eyes on them back. Surveillance and counter-surveillance, that's the name of the game.'

Is Kate aware of this? Who is ahead of whom in this deadly game?

'You do mean MI5?'

Bashir meets the question with pitying sarcasm.

'No, the Famous Five. Are you for real, brother? Our enemies have been following us for weeks.' He winks. 'They won't be watching us much longer.'

There it is again, the drumbeat of the domestic war. Majid feels as if he is walking among explosions, or the ghosts of them. All the while he looks around at the London where he grew up, at the crowds going about their routines, there is another shadow world where death awaits, ready to bleed out into these lives. Majid no longer thinks in terms of responsibility, of who cast the first stone. He had those angry words in his mouth and they choked him like marbles.

'What's going down, Bashir?'

Majid realises he may be asking too many questions too soon, inviting suspicion. Kate advised him to make his enquiries slowly, gaining Bashir's confidence, teasing his way to the truth like peeling back the layers of an onion.

'Not here. We'll talk when we reach the safe house.'

The safe house is in fact a flat on the fifteenth floor of a high-rise block in the East End. There is a mattress on the living room floor. It is ripped in one corner. There is a table and one chair. That is the sum total of the furniture. The kitchen is even more sparsely furnished. There are some kitchen units. One of the doors is missing. There is a fridge, a microwave, a cup, a plate, a knife and fork. Bashir opens the fridge to show him some ready meals and a few cans of Coke and Fanta. Bashir sees the way Majid is looking at the place.

'Not quite the Dorchester, but it should be adequate until we are ready to move you.' He waits a beat then puts his question. 'I hear Yusuf died. Was it instant?'

'Yes, he didn't know what hit him. Nobody did.'

'He died fighting a cruel enemy. Masha'Allah.'

'Why did you never go out there yourself, Bashir?'

Bashir can hear a barb in the words. His expressionless eyes study Majid's face.

'There are many ways to do God's work, my brother. My destiny lies here.'

He gestures out of the window at the carpet of lights that stretches out in every direction.

'Give me your phone.'

Majid hands it over and watches Bashir replace the SIM.

'My number is in your phone. It is the only number you will ever need.' He sees the way Majid gazes at the view. 'You like that, yeah?'

'I grew up here. It's in my heart.'

'I grew up here too. Tell me, what do you see?'

Majid hesitates. Bashir puts people to the test. Just like Omar did.

'I see the citadel of my enemies.'

Bashir smiles with satisfaction. Right answer. But Majid is telling him what he wants to hear. What he sees is home and he aches to return to his old life.

'Some people say this is the greatest city on Earth.'

It is as if he has thrown down a gauntlet to Bashir.

'This is where the infidels' pulse beats most strongly,' he retorts. 'With our guns and our suicide vests we are going to rip London's fat, sentimental heart out of its chest.'

'When?'

'What is the date today, my brother?'

Majid frowns.

'June thirtieth. Why . . .?'

Then he understands.

'That's right, Majid. A week today there is an anniversary, when our mujahideen martyred themselves in the heart of London.'

Majid feels sick.

'They boast about their security. They say never again.' He grins. 'We say *again*.'

He beats a rhythm.

'Again, again, again: until our caliphate stretches from the land of the holy places to the gates of London, Paris and Rome. Not long now, my friend.'

Then he is gone. Majid lets out a long, shuddering breath. He sweeps the flat for bugs. One of Kate's colleagues, a guy from the A2 technical division, showed him how. He declares it clean. Before long, he is picking at the stitching to release the SIM he has hidden in his waistband. He replaces the card Bashir inserted with the one he has kept concealed in his jeans. Kate answers instantly.

'They've got me in a safe house. You can locate it from my signal.'

Kate's voice crackles through the speaker.

'No need. We watched you all the way.'

'Right.'

We watched you all the way.

Of course you did. He tells her his news.

'Bashir gave me a date. Kate. I know the target, it's the seven/ seven commemoration.'

A few miles across the city Nikel is talking to Amir.

'Why don't we go and laugh at England Awakes?'

Amir turns and stares.

'Are you kidding? What if there's trouble?'

'I don't want to fight anybody, just let them know they're not welcome in this town. I thought you'd be up for it.'

'My dad would ground me for good.'

That's one reason. The other is a brother he believes is dead. Majid.

Amir nearly collides with a couple of Year Sevens careering out of the gate.

They are walking to the bus stop, checking their phones, parallel messaging. Amir is on the lookout for Nasima.

'Thing is, Nikel, your enthusiasm for this demo is a bit of a surprise. Don't take this the wrong way, but I don't have you down as a street fighter. You seem more the academic type.'

'You mean I'm a geek.'

Amir likes his new friend's honesty.

'Well, yes. That's about the size of it.'

Nikel grins.

'Who's arguing? The geeks inherit the Earth.'

The smile fades.

'Thing is, those guys see me as a soft touch. They think they can shove me around. I've had enough.'

Amir is seeing Nikel in a new light. He has never really taken him seriously until this moment.

'So you're really going to turn out for the counter-demo?'

'You bet I am. Are you going to join me?'

Amir gets a mental flashback of his father chopping with his hand to reinforce his orders.

'I can't.'

'No such thing as can't.'

'There is if you've got a dad like mine.'

'Rod of iron?'

'Got it in one.'

Only that isn't the whole picture. Amir remembers the way Majid used to barge past Dad and march out into the night, reducing his father to frustration and his mother to tears. He can hear their voices.

'Where are you going?'

'Who do you plan to meet?'

Majid never answered and there was nothing his father could do. Majid melted into the night and found something he thought was greater than himself.

'Keep making the excuses,' Nikel tells him. 'Where there's a will there's a way.'

They reach the bus stop. Nasima is there with Lucy. Lucy says something and the two girls giggle. Nikel drops his eyes self-consciously. Amir is the first to speak.

'Nikel thinks I should go to the protest on Saturday.'

Nasima's eyes widen.

'Are you crazy? Don't even think about it. What about Dad? What about Mum? Have you forgotten what they've been through?'

Nasima glances round at Lucy and Nikel.

'What's got into you, Amir? Do you want to screw everything up?'

There is no answer.

'Amir?'

'OK,' he says finally. 'I won't go.'

The twins rejoin Nikel and Lucy. They are about to board their bus when Jace puts in an appearance.

'You listen to your sister, Amir,' Jace says. 'You stay at home like a good little Paki. Saturday belongs to us.'

Amir squares up to Jace.

'What did you just call me?'

'You heard.'

He makes the shape of each letter with his mouth – P A K I – while his mates move in behind him, laughing. He takes his time over it, enjoying the effect. Nasima starts to drag her brother away.

'Ignore him, will you? He just wants to get a reaction.'

Jace hears what Nasima said and swaggers off.

'Looks like I got one.'

Nasima and Lucy jostle their way on to the bus. Nikel follows. Amir is the last to get on. He is watching Jace strolling down the road away from the stop, thinking how he would like to wipe the smile off that smug, smirking face. The demonstration just got more inviting.

THE PAST

AUTUMN, 2013

Majid had his rucksack over his right shoulder. For weeks, he had been different, a stranger in his own home. Nasima had complained that he was bullying her, demanding that she dress more modestly.

'Step aside, Dad. You can't stop me going out.'

'You are not leaving this house until you tell me where you are going.'

Amir and Nasima watched the scene. Majid was so angry. His eyes were cold and brooding.

'You can't control me, Dad. Just get out of my way.'

'You are going to meet them again, aren't you? Why do you entertain idiots who are not worth the dirt on your shoe?'

'That's it, Dad: just keep insulting my friends.'

Mum tugged at her husband's sleeve.

'Please stop shouting, Naveed. We can sort this out as a family.'

Dad was trembling with anger. He jabbed his finger at Majid.

'He is the one you should be talking to. He listens to this loudmouth Bashir more than he listens to his own parents.'

He tapped at Majid's temple, and Majid brushed his hand away in fury.

'I am not a boy, Dad. I make my own decisions.'

'And each one is crazier than the last. You spend every waking hour listening to this takfiri, this crook.'

'You know nothing about Bashir.'

'I know he is filling your head with filth. Telling you that everything wrong in the world is the fault of America and Britain. Our family came across half the world and worked hard. This country you hate gave us a home and a job.'

'And where do your taxes go, Abbu-ji? On bombs and guns to kill Muslims. They arm Israel. They rain their bombs on Gaza, Iraq and Afghanistan. They torture our brothers. They send their drones to kill us in Pakistan. Is that what you work for, to arm the Kuffar?'

'Do not use that filthy word in this house.'

Majid's face twisted.

'Oh, don't worry. I'm out of here.'

Mum stared up at him then, at the bag in his hand.

'What do you mean? Majid, where are you going?'

Dad looked terrified. Panic had replaced anger.

'No, Majid. Don't trust this man Bashir. He is an extremist. He is using you.'

'He listens to me, Dad. He takes time to explain things. I didn't know what made the world tick until I met Bashir.'

'He is filling your head full of lies.' Dad made a grab for the bag. 'You will not leave.'

Majid rushed out into the street.

Nasima was the first to react, racing to the door. 'Don't do it, Majid, please don't go!'

Majid had made his decision. He reached the street corner and turned.

He didn't look back.

THE PRESENT

FRIDAY, 1ST JULY

There are three people in the room to begin with: Kate Armstrong, a fellow member of the Counter Terrorist section called Jack Cole and their superior, Jen Sherbourne. Jen has just plucked Jack from his desk. Majid would have recognised the fourth member of the group. He joins them after a brief knock on the door. He is a tall, well-dressed Asian man.

'Before you start,' Nabil said, 'I need to bring this to your attention.'

Jen flicks through the folder, glances at Nabil, and pushes it across the table. It has the MI5 crest: *Regnum Defende.*

Defend the Realm.

Kate reads the top sheet and her heart sinks. It is Nabil's summary of what happened on the train. She tries to keep her face impassive.

'Kate, how can we trust an agent who is this easily provoked? Nabil felt he had to intervene.'

Kate stares at her fingers. It's a wonder her nails are not chewed to the quick. 'I have put months of work into this operation. I would have pulled the plug weeks ago if I thought he was unreliable.'

'Can we trust him?'

Kate remembers Majid's face as she played videos of Islamic State's atrocities across eastern Syria and western Iraq. She spared him nothing. She saw the changing emotions as his cause crumbled before her eyes.

'Kate? Is he trustworthy?'

'I believe so.'

Jen's eyes widen. She was expecting Kate to offer a stronger defence of her man.

'You *believe* so?'

'I am sure.'

Jen dismisses Nabil. 'You can go. We will take it from here.'

She turns back to Kate. 'Let me ask the question again. We have six days to avert a major incident. Think before you answer. Can he handle the stress?'

This time there is no hesitation.

'Yes.'

Jen taps her teeth with a pen.

'We have recruited an agent and placed him in the middle of London. He is in touch with two Islamist activists.'

'Three,' Kate says.

'Jamil Daud? He is just ballast. We facilitated this because we thought we could neutralise some of the most dangerous cells in the UK. We have intel of a consignment of semi-automatic rifles. God knows what else they've got in their arsenal. We have to intercept them before they fall into the wrong hands. If this goes wrong there will be serious repercussions.'

Kate knows what that means. The security forces are haunted by the events of 7 July, 2005 and other atrocities in European cities. It was the day they failed. Now there is the threat of a repeat.

Jen points out the MI5 crest on the folder. 'That's our bottom line. Take your time, Kate. I want your considered assessment.'

Kate remembers every minute she spent in Majid's company, every doubt, every twist and turn of his recruitment. She remembers one conversation in particular.

They were in a room with white walls and thin, yellow

curtains. There were two chairs and a table. The afternoon light was fading. Majid was slouched in his seat, arms thrown over the back. He was tired and increasingly impatient at the continuing interrogation. This was the time to push him to the limit in search of the truth.

'You say you want to do something. You are ready to risk your life to stop Bashir Mirza. Here's the thing: I want to be crystal clear about your motives. Not so long ago, you thought the British state was your sworn enemy. Why would you want to help us?'

He was looking at her as if she had crawled out from under a stone.

'I want the violence to stop. I want peace. Is that so hard to understand?'

'Why the sudden conversion to peace?'

'I thought I was bringing down a dictator. I went out to provide medical support. It got . . . complicated.'

Kate pursed her lips.

'Complicated? We have footage of you holding an automatic weapon.'

'It was self-defence: kill or be killed. Have you seen what a barrel bomb can do?'

'Don't try to shift the argument, Majid. There is footage of you standing over bound men. That is hardly self-defence. What made you walk away?'

Majid persisted in his explanation.

'I was unable to make a difference out there in Syria. It was utter horror.'

Still Kate picked away at everything he said.

'You took up arms. You chose to go to war. You were willing to kill.'

'I wanted to fight the dictator, not my own brothers. I wanted to defend women and children, not . . .'

'Not abuse them.'

'Yes.'

'You decided Bashir had used you?'

Majid's face twisted, as if in pain.

'He lied to me. Misled me. Betrayed me. He made me feel like a hero, put me on a pedestal; then he threw me to the ground. All I found out there was blood and shame.'

Kate knew it was time to go for the kill.

'But you think you can make a difference at home?'

'Maybe.' There was a hesitation. 'I can do something you can't. I can find the man you want.'

'Bashir is intent on bloodshed. Can you help us stop him?'

'Yes.'

Everything hinged on Kate's judgement.

'Kate?'

Jen's voice scatters her memories, pulling her back into the room in Thames House. Kate knows what to say.

'Bungee is ours. He is sickened by what he saw in Syria. He had a young man's dream. It didn't turn out the way he expected.'

Jen's face gives nothing away. After three decades in the service she has learned to play her cards close to her chest.

'That doesn't make him a loyal servant to the British state.'

'Can I speak frankly, Jen?'

'Feel free.'

'I have heard you criticise the war on terror yourself. You said it was a blunt instrument.'

Jen is not fazed.

'What's your point, Kate?'

'If you, a senior figure in state security, can think the war *on* terror became a war *of* terror . . .'

Jen's face registers displeasure.

'I never went that far, Kate.'

'OK, if you think the war on terror is part of the reason for the problems we have now, imagine how a young Muslim feels.'

'Don't preach to me, Kate, and don't make excuses for your protégé. I am aware that your sympathies are on the liberal end of the spectrum. The war on terror does not excuse violent extremism. Let's cut to the chase. Convince me that Bungee is still our man.'

Kate makes her pitch.

'He went to Syria to protect women and children. In however distorted a way, he thought he was fighting oppression. He saw himself as somebody who was on the side of the angels.'

Jen interrupts.

'He fought alongside militants who would go on to butcher innocents. Would you like me to list their crimes: the beheadings, the torture, the massacres, the abuse of women?'

Kate glances at Jack for support. For now, he holds his peace.

Kate continues, 'Bungee believed in a cause, like millions of others throughout history. Bashir Mirza convinced him of that cause and it became a nightmare. He hates his former mentor for that.'

Finally, Jack speaks. Kate has always had him down as somebody who placed his career before his convictions. To her surprise, he is on her side.

'Bungee has put his neck on the line, reporting Bashir's plans to us. I trust Kate's judgement.'

'You've read Nabil's report?'

'I have, and I have spoken to Nabil about it. There are signs of instability, that's true, but this is a young guy. Bungee is under stress. Who wouldn't be shaky in the circumstances?'

'So you concur with Kate? We take his words on face value?'

Jack appears to consider the question carefully before answering.

'Yes.'

Jen nods.

'Fine. Let's get to work.'

10

Rose Cottage is set back from a country lane, along an uneven track. In this part of rural Hertfordshire there are farms, an equestrian centre and a number of B&Bs. They are a mile away. There is nobody to watch the comings and goings. Rose Cottage belongs to a local farmer. He let it out to a smartly dressed, well-spoken man in his early thirties, somebody in financial difficulties and grateful for the generous amount of cash he received for making the booking. Its occupants are two Asian men: Jamil and Bashir. The third member of the group is a man of Nigerian descent, David, who prefers to use the nom de guerre Abu Rashid. After breakfast and prayers, Abu Rashid opens the door, gets in the car and drives off without a word.

'Where's he going?'

Bashir watches the car bumping along the track towards the lane before replying to Jamil.

'He's got things to do.'

Jamil isn't satisfied with that.

'I'm the last man standing.'

Bashir stiffens and turns round.

'What?'

'I'm talking about the little group you put together back in the day. There were four of us when we first met, Bashir. Yusuf, Majid and yours truly. Now it's just you and me.'

There is an edge to his voice. Jamil would never be bold enough to accuse Bashir of using him, but there is a hint of accusation in his tone. What Jamil wants is trust. Bashir interprets his words differently.

'Do you wish you had chosen martyrdom like them? I offered to help with your passage.'

Jamil sidesteps the question.

'They both got to fight. People will remember them. All I do is sit around places like this.'

Bashir points out of the window at a sunlit valley.

'When did you ever sit around somewhere like this before, city boy?'

It is true, of course. The rural scene before them might as well be an alien landscape. Jamil has spent his entire life in the estates of inner London, amid the traffic congestion, streetlights and wail of sirens. The first night here he stood marvelling at the star-studded sky, wondering how there could be so many winking lights in the heavens. He felt tiny and insignificant before the majesty of the universe. Now he feels equally insignificant in Bashir's eyes.

'You keep telling me we're going to hit back at the enemy, make the world sit up and notice, but nothing ever happens.'

Bashir sits down, crosses his legs and folds his arms.

'Something will happen. Soon.'

'That's it? Soon? I'm not some stupid kid.'

Bashir uncrosses his legs, plants his feet apart and rests his arms on his thighs. He leans forward, scrutinising Jamil, lips forming a tight, ill-tempered line.

'So you want to know what's going down?'

'You want me to be a mujahid. I deserve to know.'

Bashir nods, head and shoulders moving slowly.

'Fine. All I have to say is seven/seven.'

Jamil takes a moment to understand.

'We're going to hit the anniversary?'

'Got it in one, Einstein. We are ready, Jamil.'

Bashir glances at the calendar on the wall. It hasn't been changed since March. He tears off the pages until he comes to July.

'We will make it the month of the martyrs.'

THE PAST

WINTER, 2013

Majid braced himself and turned the key in the lock. He breathed a sigh of relief when he entered an empty house. Bashir called from the car.

'Get the rest of your stuff. We've things to do.'

Majid nodded and jogged upstairs. He went straight to the drawer and rummaged around until he found his passport. That's when he heard Bashir hit the horn. By the time he had reached the foot of the stairs there was Dad.

He took a step forward.

'I saw Bashir outside.'

'Let's not quarrel, Dad. I just came back for some stuff.'

Dad looked suspicious.

'What stuff? Your hands are empty.'

'Dad, I'm going.'

As he tried to push past, Dad grabbed his sleeve.

'Don't walk away, Majid. You are breaking your mother's heart.'

Dad picked up a letter from the hall table.

'This is from the university. You've been missing lectures. What do you think you're doing? You are throwing your whole life down the toilet.'

'Bashir is my university now, Dad. I'm learning things you never told me.'

A frown darkened his father's features.

'What are you talking about? What can you learn from a cheap gangster?'

Majid shook his head.

'You can't even imagine, can you? I am learning about the Americans and their Zionist-crusader allies. I am learning about the apostate Gulf Arab states. They're the global gangsters. I never understood why Muslims were targeted until now.'

'What is wrong with you, Majid? You are talking in slogans.'

'I am telling the truth, Dad. Live your life of obedience if you like, but I will not stand by while my Muslim brothers and sisters are slaughtered.'

His father persists.

'Stay. Your mother is worried.'

'This isn't home any more. For the first time in my life I have a purpose. I mean something.'

Majid's words provoked a groan of dismay from his father.

'You always meant something. You are my son. That man is brainwashing you.'

Majid shrugged him away.

'I will make my jihad my own way, Abbu-ji.'

Horror filled his father's eyes.

'Jihad. You don't know the meaning of the word. What are you saying?'

'There is an obligation to defend women and children. I have skills. I can save lives.'

'You have only studied medicine for two years. What do you think you can do? Majid, this is madness.'

'Do you want to know what madness really is?' Majid retorted. 'It is madness to live quietly in the house of your enemy while your brothers and sisters die. London is a prison. I feel as if I have a noose round my neck. What is there here for me? I want freedom, honour. I want my life to mean something.'

Majid had opened the front door now, and he and his father were standing on the step. He was aware of Bashir watching from the car. His mentor didn't like the raised voices, drawing the attention of neighbours. Majid's voice faltered and he looked round at Bashir.

'We need to go.'

THE PRESENT

||

FRIDAY, 1ST JULY

Abu Rashid is back. He senses a problem and flashes a silent question with his eyes. Bashir raises a finger to his lips.

'I'm going to tell you something. Don't react.'

Abu Rashid glances at Jamil then back at Bashir.

'What is this? Why are the curtains closed?'

Bashir tugs at the corner of the curtain.

'We've got company. See those trees? There's a surveillance team in the lane beyond.'

'Special Branch?'

'Most likely Five. I saw one of them earlier.'

'Do they know they're rumbled?'

'I don't think so. My guess is it's just a watching brief. There won't be a raid unless there is something to find. Now to business. The consignment, did you see it?'

Abu Rashid is sweating.

'Yes, the packages have come.'

'Packages?' Jamil says, glancing from Abu Rashid to Bashir. 'What packages?'

Abu Rashid produces his phone and brings up a photo. It shows a machine pistol.

'It's the guns. I got to see a sample.'

Bashir scowls.

'You took a photo? You were meant to check the quality of the merchandise and that's all.' He seems twitchy. 'Not a word until we've got some background noise.'

He turns the TV on. Loud. The three men cluster round, keeping their voices low. Abu Rashid's eyes betray a measure of excitement.

'To be specific,' Abu Rashid continues, 'I got to see a Škorpion vz.Sixty-one sub-machine-gun. These babies are light and easy to use. More importantly, you can carry them like pistols. They're perfect.'

Jamil stares excitedly at the photo.

'Have you got the guns?'

Abu Rashid and Bashir react visibly. Abu Rashid registers his irritation.

'Not with me. Do I look like I was born yesterday? I got to examine a sample. The rest are going into storage now the deal is made. Only Bashir knows where.'

Jamil pounces on the admission.

'So Bashir doesn't trust you either?'

Bashir reaches out and taps Jamil's forehead with his finger.

'Only one member of the cell gets to know the location of the weapons. It's basic security.'

'I was only asking.'

Bashir gives Jamil's shoulder a bump.

'What's with all the questions? I thought we'd told you, everything is on a need-to-know basis. *I* need to know.' It's his turn to jab Jamil with his finger. 'You don't.'

His eyes stray around the walls of the cottage and he wags a finger at his surroundings. 'This has all been swept for devices, yeah?'

Abu Rashid looks insulted.

'I told you. We didn't give Five a chance to bug the place. It's clean.' He glances outside. 'We're out of range of any listening devices.'

'Are you sure about that?'

'I'm sure.'

12

Kate is processing the information that has just come in from the surveillance team: snatches of poor quality chatter picked up by a bug, grainy long-distance shots of Abu Rashid arriving, earlier CCTV footage of him having a meet with two men, both unidentified. It is confirmation of what Majid told her. She circles a couple of words from the patchy script: July, martyrs, packages. They all add up to one thing.

Terrorist status: Critical.

Risk of attack imminent.

A call interrupts her train of thought. It's Majid.

'You must be a mind-reader.'

'Come again?'

His voice is shaky, fractious.

'Are you OK?'

'Kate, I don't know if I can do this. Bashir is suspicious.'

'Suspicious how?'

Majid is on edge. There is no mistaking his unease.

'OK, it's just a gut feeling. It's the way he looks at me.'

Kate moves to reassure him. The material on her desk says Majid is more important than ever. They have a date. They need a time and place. She has to be in control. Without Majid, Five will be whistling in the dark and the attack could be days away. The surveillance team had eyes on Abu Rashid, but he lost them in a shopping mall. Bashir Mirza's team is always one step ahead. Its members slip out of sight for hours at an end, but Five's resources are stretched.

'Can you give me concrete proof that he suspects you?'

'No. It's just a feeling. Kate, I've got to get out of here.'

Kate's been here before. Irritable Agent Syndrome.

'No, you don't, Majid. What you're doing takes courage, but it's the right thing. You know that, don't you?'

'Do I?'

'Bashir wants to kill and maim innocent people. You said you wanted to stop him.'

Majid is over the worst.

'OK, OK.'

He is back from the brink. She can steady him. She has to.

'Have you done anything to make him suspect you?'

This time the reply is prompt. Kate sucks in a deep breath. She has stemmed Majid's slide into panic.

'No, nothing. I'm not stupid.'

'Then you need to relax. We're watching you.' She doesn't mention the way they were watching Abu Rashid and lost him. 'We're here for you, you've got to believe that.'

She wants him to know the service is his support system. He has to believe. He distrusts the security services as an institution so he has to have faith in his handler. The sense of attachment is crucial. 'There is an A4 surveillance team watching your every move. We are ready to move in at a moment's notice. You've got time on your hands. Try not to dwell on things.'

She can hear the suppressed anger in Majid's voice.

'That's easy for you to say. I'm the one in the hot seat.'

Kate concentrates on steadying his nerves.

'This is the worst time, when you are waiting for things to happen. It's natural that you're a bit worried, but we've got your back.'

She wonders whether she is reassuring him too much, but he barely notices. She goes on, 'We'll be with you every step of the way. We walked you through it, remember?'

They are beginning to go over the same ground.

'Have there been any more developments, any clues about the target?'

'No. Bashir is keeping me in the dark. I just can't help feeling they know something.'

That again.

'It doesn't mean they're suspicious of you. This is the whole purpose of a cell structure. Decision-making lies with the fewest number possible. Leaks are minimised.'

'OK.' Majid's voice is calmer. 'What about my family? You promised to keep an eye on them. I need to know they're safe.'

Kate has been here before, trying to reassure an asset when there is nothing she can do. It makes her skin crawl every time, but her job is to save lives. She has no new information about his family. She made the usual promises, but resources are stretched thinly and it isn't a priority. She doesn't tell him any of this. There is no point.

'Your family is doing just fine.'

She delivers the line with flawless confidence, in spite of the fact that she has had no contact with the Sarwars.

'You have to clear your mind. Everything depends on you remaining calm and focused. Your safety is my priority. Nothing is going to go wrong.'

There. Another promise. Easy to make. Harder to keep. *This is your job, Katie girl. Remember your priorities.*

'You're sure about that?'

'I am quite sure. Stay in touch if you can, but don't take any risks. Have you got that?'

'I hear you.'

When Majid hangs up, Kate puts her head in her hands.

'OK,' she tells herself, 'the Sarwars go on the back burner.'

THE PRESENT

13

SATURDAY, 2ND JULY

'What's wrong, Mum? You look worried.'

'Your father and I have got to go to Luton. Nanny Ammi has had a fall. We are picking up Fatima and Rabia on the way.'

They are halfway out of the door when Dad turns round.

'And no sneaking out to that march. You stay in, hear? If there was room in the car, I would take you two with me.' He pulls out his phone. 'I will be calling to check.'

'Yes, Abbu-ji.'

Nasima goes to the window and watches them go. As the car pulls away, Amir starts texting. Nasima turns to her brother.

'What are you doing?'

'Come on, Nas. This is fate.'

Her skin prickles.

'You mean you're going to the march, after everything you promised? Amir, you can't!'

His mind is clearly made up.

'They won't be finished in Luton until late. I'll be well back.'

'You heard what Dad said. He's going to call.'

'He won't ring for a couple of hours. There's time. Cover for me. You've done it before.'

'Amir, you can't. Have you forgotten what happened to Majid?'

'How is this the same, Nas? He went to Syria to make jihad.'

'It's trouble. This is how it starts.'

Amir shakes his head.

'This is how it ends. We're going to chase those Nazis off the streets.'

'If something goes wrong, you'll break our parents' hearts.'

'Nothing is going to go wrong. Trust me.'

Nasima is still trying to persuade Amir when his phone rings.

'Hi. You got my text? Yes, I'll see you down there.' He pockets the phone and turns to Nasima.

'Was that Nikel?'

Amir is beaming.

'Yes, he's there. He says there's a couple of hundred people already, waiting for the racists to show up.'

He hurries to get his jacket, and Nasima rushes after him.

'Listen to me. What do I say if you're not back when Dad phones?'

'Tell him I'm in the bath.'

'Amir, this is crazy.'

He shrugs into the jacket and walks to the door.

'Stop worrying, will you?'

Nasima hasn't stopped worrying since the night she saw Bashir and her father quarrelling on the drive.

'Amir.' Her voice follows him down the stairs. 'Amir!'

14

'Listen.'

The England Awakes marchers, still out of sight, are singing, football-style. The first chant ends with the word 'England'.

'Look. They're using mounted police.'

Two police officers on horseback follow the van. They are wearing black crash helmets with visors.

'Look at that: even the horses have got hi-vis jackets.'

'That's to stop them getting lost in the crowd.'

Laughter travels around the crowd, but it is the nervous variety. The numbers opposing England Awakes amount to fewer than five hundred. There is another raucous chant from the top of the road.

'We want our country back! We want our country back!'

Several heads are visible now. Most are wearing baseball caps or have their heads and faces covered by hoods and scarves. More police in hi-vis jackets line the march, forming a pale green border. There is a new chant coming from England Awakes.

'Whose streets? Our streets!'

A big guy, one of the crowd defending the mosque, objects. He thrusts his hands into the air and roars to the rest of the counter-demonstration.

'Did you hear them? That's our slogan, not theirs.'

He gives the lead, bellowing at the top of his voice.

'Do these streets belong to racists?'

The crowd roars in response:

'No!'

'Is it a white street?'

'No!'

'Is it a black street?'

'No!'

'Is it a Muslim street?'

Most of the crowd shouts no. A few of the boys shout yes, followed by ironic laughter. Some of them start up a chant.

'Jihad, jihad.'

'You can knock that off,' Big Guy says. 'This is a united community protest, not a religious thing.'

Grudgingly, the boys stop. Big Guy leads the counter-chant.

'Whose streets? *Our streets!*'

The England Awakes march is approaching. Banners sway. Fists punch towards the sky. There is excitement in the air. Suddenly, the anger and the shouting are replaced by another sound. Laughter.

Amir frowns. 'What's so funny?'

Nikel grabs his shoulder.

'Turn round. That's what they're laughing at.'

The England Awakes march is coming round a bend in the road. For the first time it is possible to make a guess at numbers. There are no more than eighty people on the march. As somebody yells:

'You could get them all on a double-decker bus.'

15

Nasima is sitting at the window, chin resting on her arms. Amir is still not home. Her stomach is in knots as she sits waiting for the phone to ring. She knows her parents will call. It is Amir's fault, but she is the one who is going to have to face the music. She turns on her laptop to see if there is any news of the march. The only search results are articles published in the run-up to the demonstration. She turns the radio on. It is ten minutes until the bulletin.

'Where are you, Amir? This isn't fair.'

She tries calling him, but his phone is switched off. She sends a text, the fourth since he left.

Ring me.

Please.

He doesn't phone, not in the next minute, not in the next five or ten. Just before the hour, Nasima turns on the radio.

'*Rival demonstrations are confronting each other outside Central Mosque. Some one hundred England Awakes marchers are holding a rally, while a larger counter-demonstration of some four hundred people faces them across Hill Street. The atmosphere is noisy, but largely peaceful. Other news . . .*'

Nasima switches off. *Largely peaceful.* Is that the same as completely peaceful? There was no mention of arrests. That's got to be good. Her phone goes, but it isn't Amir. It's Lucy.

Nasima can hear noise in the background.

'I thought you didn't want anything to do with the march?'

'It was passing right outside my house. I had to see.'

'What's happening?'

'It's so funny. There's only about fifty of them . . .'

'The news said a hundred.'

'No way! Fifty might be a bit of an underestimate, but no way are there a hundred of them. That's ridiculous.'

'Have you seen Amir?'

'Yes, he's over there with Nikel.'

So he's still there.

'Have you spoken to him? Did you give him my message? He's got to turn his phone on!'

'I gave him your message, Nas.'

'And?'

'And nothing. I tried. I don't think he wants to talk to you.'

Nasima is numb with disappointment.

'Oh well, you tried, Luce. Thank you. Stay safe, won't you?'

'Of course.'

'See you in school.'

She hangs up and decides to get something to eat. She is on the way into the kitchen when the phone goes. This time it's Dad.

'Is everything all right, Nasima?'

Nasima wonders how she is meant to answer. She goes for positive.

'Yes, of course it is. How's Nanny Ammi?'

'She's fine. She's just got to rest for a few days.'

'What time are you getting home?'

'About ten o'clock, I think. It depends on the traffic.' He pauses. 'Your mother wants to know if you have eaten?'

Nasima smiles. That's Mum.

'I'm making something now.' She takes a chance. 'I'm going to have some dhal – with Amir.'

71

Nasima feels like hugging herself. *See what I did there?*

'So he's there? I was concerned he might go to that demonstration.'

Something about the ensuing silence makes Dad suspicious.

'Nasima, he is there, isn't he?'

She remembers what Amir said.

'Yes, he's in the bath.'

'Very well. I will call back in ten minutes.'

'There's no need, Abbu-ji. I'll tell him you called.'

'That's for me to decide, Nasima. I will call back in ten minutes.'

Nasima cancels the call and tries Amir again. His number is still unavailable. She phones Lucy.

'Luce, give Amir this message immediately. Tell him Dad is calling home in ten minutes. He's got to be here when Dad phones back.'

After that, she sits at the kitchen table, no longer hungry, staring at her phone, waiting for it to ring again. *Let it be Amir,* she pleads. *Or Lucy.* Finally, it rings. It's her father.

'Hi Dad. He's still in the bath.'

'I'm not sure I believe you, Nasima.' A pause. 'OK, if he's in the bath, take the phone to the bathroom door and tell him to shout a message to me. I will be able to hear him.'

It is obvious that her father is not going to give up.

'Be honest with me, Nasima. Is he there?'

Nasima's resolve collapses.

'I'm so sorry, Dad. I couldn't stop him.'

16

Taunts and laughter are echoing around the crossroads. Jubilant at the tiny turnout of the England Awakes march, the counter-demonstrators press forward, crowding round the police lines. They want to rub their opponents' noses in the embarrassment of a much-advertised March of a Thousand that has failed even to reach three figures.

'What's this,' somebody calls, 'the million-man march?'

'Maybe it's the one-brain-cell march.'

'Excuse me,' another voice shouts, 'I can see at least two brain cells. Oh no, sorry: double vision.'

The jokes keep coming. The effect on the England Awakes marchers is sudden and dramatic. They start to throw themselves against the cordon of police, trying to reach their tormentors. Soon demonstrator and counter-demonstrator are jabbing fingers and yelling insults over the heads and shoulders of the police. The police have their backs to the England Awakes supporters. They glare at the counter-demonstrators. Amir finds himself being pushed to the front, but he doesn't resist. Instead, he turns towards Nikel, eyes glittering with excitement.

'Whose streets?' he laughs. 'Our streets.'

Enraged by the mocking taunts of the counter-demonstrators, the England Awakes marchers start pelting their opponents with anything they can lay their hands on: cans, stones, coins. A bottle smashes at Amir's feet. He shouts a protest at the nearest police officer.

'Aren't you going to stop them?'

'Things will soon be flying from both sides, son,' the copper grunts. 'We're here to keep the two sides apart.'

A stone thumps into Amir's shoulder without causing any serious damage.

'Did you see that?' Amir yells. 'Why aren't you arresting them?'

The copper glances over his shoulder just as the counter-demonstrators start retaliating with missiles of their own.

'See what I mean?'

Amir isn't satisfied. He is jabbing fingers at the England Awakes marchers.

'But they started it. This is self-defence.'

Nikel is at Amir's side.

'Cut it out, will you? There's no point arguing with the police. We outnumber the goons. We've won. What are you getting so angry for?'

He doesn't know about Majid. He doesn't understand the emotions exploding in Amir's chest. A year of grief and rage boil up in Amir. For so long he has been struggling with the hurt and bewilderment of losing a brother the way he did, in a barely comprehensible war in a distant land. He has seen his life fall apart. For months he has wanted to lash out, to break something. Two burly England Awakes stewards see Amir and focus their taunts on him.

'What's up, Terror Boy?' one of them yells. 'Don't you like the truth? England for the English.'

The second man keeps it simple.

'Paki.'

Amir hears the racism that turned Majid, the hostility that made him look for a war to fight.

The men can see their words are having an impact.

'Not all Muslims are terrorists, but all terrorists are Muslims.'

Amir hears the drumbeat of a score of media headlines. Muslim. Terrorist. He relives the news of Majid's death. Muslim. Terrorist. He wants to ram their words down their throats.

'Nazi scum, Nazi scum!'

The cop's eyes narrow.

'Just calm down.'

The stewards have got him where they want him.

'Terror Boy.'

Amir is beside himself, screaming at them until he can feel his own spit on his chin. The cop is losing patience.

'I won't tell you again.'

Now he has the men's faces sneering in front of him. He has the words of a police force Majid told him were their enemies. He turns and screams his hatred in the cop's face. The reaction is instant. The officer makes a grab for Amir.

'Right you, that's it.'

Amir feels his arms being forced back and starts to struggle. Now he has another arm round his neck and shoulders. He is being propelled through the crowd. Faces blur as he stumbles forward. Shouts burst around him. From his left, a punch is thrown. He doesn't know whether it is at him or at the police. A hand is pushing down on his skull. He understands. He has seen this in a hundred crime dramas. It is to protect his head as they bundle him into the van.

He is under arrest.

17

The Sarwar family is looking at the photograph of Amir being arrested. Dad presses his fingers against his eyebrows, trying to rub away the shame. They have been discussing Amir's arrest for an hour and everybody is tired.

'What were you thinking?'

Nasima tries to interrupt.

'Dad, is this really necessary?'

Dad's stare is hard and unyielding.

'Is it necessary? Nasima, your brother has been arrested. The police have made the link with Majid. They want to refer him to the Prevent strategy.'

'Prevent? That's to stop terrorism.'

'Exactly. They think he has been *radicalised*.'

He does the speech mark thing with his fingers. Amir reacts as if he has been electrocuted.

'All I did was go on a march.'

Dad stabs a finger at his son.

'Enough! You have no right to raise your voice to me. Who came to get you out of the police station? I did. Who told the police that you were a good boy, a hard-working student who had a bright future ahead of him?'

Amir scowls.

'Cheers, Dad. You really sound like you meant it.'

Mum takes his hand.

'Please, Amir. This has been a shock for us.'

Amir snatches his hand from his mother in frustration.

'What, and you think it's been a picnic for me? The police dragged me through a crowd of racists. That's how I got this.' He points to the discoloured mark on his cheek. 'They let those thugs have a free shot at me. Now I'm an "at-risk individual". What else was it? Oh yes, I'm *vulnerable*.'

Mum glances at her husband.

'Does the school have to know? His exams are only a month away. All the disruption has made it hard for him to revise as it is.'

Dad doesn't answer. Instead, he cold-eyes his son. Amir takes the hint and explains for his mother's benefit.

'The police have already been in touch with the school. They're going to teach me fundamental British values, you know the kind of thing: tell me all about red postboxes and Routemaster buses.'

Mum frowns. 'They think Amir is some kind of trainee terrorist?'

Dad sighs. 'I didn't want to upset you. When I was in that room with Amir and the police officers, I felt as if I was under scrutiny too. They kept asking me about Majid. When did I know something was wrong? Were there any danger signs? Did he have any extremist literature in his room? What websites did he visit? Did I examine his internet history? Then they put the same questions about Amir. They made me feel like a criminal.'

Amir nods.

'You and me both, Dad.'

'There is a difference, Amir. I didn't get myself arrested. Listen to me very carefully. You listen to every word I say. You are going to do whatever they want. You will say Yes sir, No sir, Three rotten bags full, sir. You will stay out of trouble. By the time you have done your exams, we should have sold the house. Then, finally, we can put this and Majid behind us . . .'

He hesitates, realising that isn't what he meant to say. 'We will get through this and start over. We will survive.'

18

Jamil misses Majid. He misses the good times with him and Yusuf. They were brothers. They grew up together, took everything life could throw at them together, got angry together. Jamil remembers the night they made their decision. It was Yusuf who threw out the challenge.

'Syria's where it's happening. They're calling it the Fourth Reich, the worst since Hitler. Ten thousand killed in custody. They're torturing people out there, electrocuting them, ripping out their fingernails. They're reducing cities to rubble. Bashir says he knows people. They'll sort out all the arrangements. I'm up for it. Who's with me?'

'You mean . . . go out there?'

'Why not?'

Jamil closed his eyes. He was the one who had to say no.

'My mum's sick, yeah? She's got cancer. I can't come with you.'

Yusuf didn't understand. What's one sick mother compared to millions suffering?

'You're making excuses. What about you, Majid? Still think helping out at this charity of yours is enough? Still think boxes of food and medicine are going to bring down Assad?'

'When did I ever think that?'

'You put your heart and soul into the collections.'

Majid rubs his nose.

'Yes, and I'm proud of the work I've done. I am not going to pick up a gun, but I can work out there as a medic.'

Yusuf's eyes blazed with excitement.

'You mean it? We're going to do it?'

Majid nodded slowly, as if only now realising what he had agreed to. It was as if he was sleepwalking.

'Yes, we're going to do it.'

Jamil stands in the doorway, remembering the sound of Majid's voice, slow and distracted at first, then louder and stronger.

They're dead, but the war goes on. Jamil murmurs his personal pledge to those responsible.

'I'm going to avenge my brothers. I'm going to bring the war home.'

THE PAST

SPRING, 2014

The sky was dimming, turning to ink. Majid felt dizzy. It was hard to believe it was really happening, but the landscape before him was unlike anything in London. The ground was stony and treacherous. In the distance, there were olive groves. Until that moment, everything had gone as Bashir told them it would: the arrival at Istanbul Atatürk Airport, the transfer to Antakya, the Turkish name for the ancient city of Antioch. The streets of the town were busy. Yusuf's Arabic was better than Majid's. He made it his business to talk to some of the men they met. He identified Yemenis, Saudis, even a German-born Iraqi. An hour's drive brought them to the border.

'Is this it?'

Their driver waved them forward. They had to pay him double to get this far.

'Bashir said somebody would meet us here.'

There was a shrug from the driver.

'I don't know any Bashir.'

There were knots of people on the hillside to their left and right.

'Yallah. Move. Hurry up.'

Majid noticed three silhouetted figures watching them from the Turkish side of the border.

'Who are they?'

He felt a hand on his shoulder and turned to see a man in his thirties, grinning at him.

'That's the gendarmes,' said the man. 'Somebody has probably bribed them to let us cross the border. Stop dawdling or they might change their mind. Did you come to join the revolution?'

'We came to make our jihad.'

The smile faded from the man's face.

'Have you got Syrian blood?'

Yusuf stepped in.

'His people are from the Punjab.' He bent and picked up a handful of soil. 'This is my land.'

'Where is your family from?'

'Hama.'

The newcomer seemed happy with that. He offered his hand.

'I am Mahmoud. Come with me.'

THE PRESENT

19

SUNDAY, 3RD JULY

Bashir calls. Less than a minute later he is at the door. Majid hears him kicking it and opens up. He sees why Bashir didn't use his key. He has carrier bags in both hands. Majid can smell the aroma of a takeaway and his stomach growls.

'OK, you've got food. What's this other stuff?'

'Clothes and a pair of shoes.'

'What's wrong with the gear I've got on?'

'This is security. Five can put bugs in shoes, all kinds of stuff. Did you never see *Enemy of the State*?'

'Will Smith? That wasn't MI5.'

'MI5's got that sort of equipment, that's what I'm saying.'

Majid feels his scalp crawl. Bashir's paranoia would be comic if it wasn't for the SIM in his waistband.

'Don't you trust me, Bashir?'

'This is a precaution. We're about to move. Everybody follows the same rules.'

'Even you?'

'Even me. Five's running an agent.'

Bashir shoves the pile of clothes at him.

'Get changed.' He laughs. 'Call this battledress.'

Majid sets off for the bathroom. His heart is slamming. Kate's words flutter through his mind.

We've got your back.

It doesn't feel like that. Here, with Bashir, he feels utterly exposed, hung out to dry.

'No, get changed here, where I can see you.'

Now it isn't just Majid's scalp that's crawling. His skin is prickling all over.

Majid nods and starts to undress. It is as if he is peeling away every layer of protection. His mind is racing. What if Bashir sees Kate's SIM?

'What's wrong? Turning shy on me?'

Bashir chuckles and Majid forces a reciprocal laugh before taking off his trainers then stripping to his underpants. Majid bundles his clothes together, desperately feeling for the SIM. He can't find it. What the hell?

'Something wrong?'

Majid is scanning the floor.

'No, I thought I had a stick of chewing gum in the pocket. Must have gone through it already.'

Bashir nods.

'Chewing is good for the nerves. By the end of this, you'll have jaws like a hyena.'

Majid watches as Bashir runs his hands over the jeans, shirt, even the socks and T-shirt. That's when he sees the SIM. A crackle of fright goes through him. It is lying on the floor between them. It must have fallen out when he was changing. Has Bashir seen? If he has, Majid is a dead man. Suddenly, it is as if that tiny piece of black plastic is throbbing, growing, taking up the whole floor.

Majid takes a chance and thrusts his trainers towards Bashir for him to examine next. With Bashir occupied, Majid slides his bare foot across the floor and places it on the small, black card. He feels it stick. He continues to dress in the new set of clothes, praying the SIM will cling to his skin. He pulls on his socks and ties his laces. It's still there.

Alhamdulillah.

Thanks be to God.

Bashir turns to leave.

'Five days and counting, Majid. Next time you see me, we go to war.'

With Bashir gone, Majid has time to think. There are two possibilities. One, Bashir was telling the truth. They make sure everybody is clean, just as a precaution. Two, he is under suspicion. That means Bashir could have planted a bug.

Think, Majid tells himself. *What did Bashir do? Where did he go? He stood here, in the middle of the floor space. I looked away while I was dressing. Could he have planted anything?* Majid examines the room, running his fingers along surfaces, peering under units.

Nothing.

He wonders if he can take a chance. He is late calling Kate. What if they pull the operation? There is a stash of machine guns out there somewhere. At least one other cell is at large. The idea sickens him.

It is hard to concentrate. Majid's thoughts fly about without making any sense. He stands there for at least a minute. Finally, he takes off his shoe and sock, pulls out the SIM, puts it back in the phone and makes the call. There is nothing to tell. The call is routine, the routine of madness. Majid hangs on to Kate's voice like a man clinging to driftwood.

'Anything to report?' she asks.

'It's still on.'

After the call, he swaps the SIMs, puts his sock and shoe back on. He is trembling. He makes his way back into the flat and washes his face with cold water. Droplets of moisture glint in his beard. His eyes are bleak and hard. They have witnessed too much.

And it isn't over yet.

It has only just begun.

20

Amir joins the rest of the family in the living room.

'Sulk over?' Nasima whispers.

He gives her the dead eye then pinches her forearm.

'Hey, that hurt!'

They get the parental stare, but nobody wants to rock the boat. They are done with shouting for one day. It is a fine evening outside. Sunlight shimmers along the far wall of the room. Four pairs of eyes are fixed on the TV but nobody is watching. Once more, it is Nasima who speaks first. She leans across to her mother.

'Have you spoken to Nanny Ammi tonight?'

'She's on the mend. It wasn't too serious a fall. Nothing broken, just bruising. You know what she's like. It is killing her to sit still and have everybody fussing over her.'

Amir turns round.

'Does she know about my arrest?'

'We had to tell her.'

Amir lays his head on the back of the couch and stares at the ceiling.

'I'm sorry, Ammi-ji. You too, Abbu-ji.'

Dad comes to a decision.

'No, I didn't handle it well. Instead of shouting and yelling, I should have listened. The last eighteen months have been hard on you.' He sits forward. 'Look, I find it difficult to talk about Majid. So many times, I sat in judgement on other parents, passed comment on their children. I should have been more humble. What kind of father am I to have a son like Majid?'

'Dad . . .'

'No, hear me out. Every day I wonder if there is something I could have said or done. What made Majid change? We had a son who did well at school, was training to become a doctor. I thought our job was done. He was a success, a boy to be proud of. Was it those friends of his? He never stopped hanging out with them. Was I too strict, too lenient?'

'You tried, Abbu-ji. He wouldn't listen.'

'I should have asked for help. Pride is a terrible flaw. I acted so high and mighty and I have fallen a long way.'

Mum goes over to him. She kneels next to his chair and rests a hand on his arm.

'Nobody is judging you, Naveed. You are a good man. You did everything you could. We both did. Sometimes . . . I don't know . . . maybe sometimes, no matter what you do, your children have to make their own decisions, whether they are right or wrong. Majid was a wonderful boy, but he wasn't perfect. He was always wilful, so headstrong and stubborn.'

'A bit like me?'

She smiles.

'Yes, like you. He was always so angry at injustice. It made him compassionate for others, but it created a rage inside him. That's what made him go.'

'I just wish they could have returned his body. It is so hard not knowing about his last moments.'

'It will have been painless, Naveed. Death in a rocket attack is sudden.'

'Yes, at least he is at peace.'

'He is at peace. Alhamdulillah.'

21

Kate is working overtime. Everybody is in a high state of tension. The evening news has confirmed what the security services already knew; that the Home Secretary has raised the alert from Severe to Critical. There is a knock on the door.

'Come in.'

Jen enters the room. She does not make eye contact.

'You wanted to talk to me, Kate?'

'It's Bungee. He was late calling in.'

'How late?'

Kate is feeling uncomfortable.

'Two hours.'

'Did you ask him why?'

'No, he's brittle enough as it is. I thought I might push him over the edge.'

'What's the word from the A4 team?'

'Bashir Mirza called in at the flat earlier. He had bags with him. One was from a convenience store, one of those Twenty Four Seven places. The others were from a clothes shop. Jeans, T-shirts, a shoe box.'

Jen considers the information.

'It sounds as if our boys are ready to move. We'd better be on our toes.'

Jen takes a seat, crosses her legs and checks her watch.

That she stays to talk is an indication that she is taking Kate's concerns seriously.

'We have all the main players under surveillance. We are ready to move in at any time. Bungee could hardly be safer.' Her eyes fix on Kate. 'Or are you wondering if we're safe with him?'

Kate asked Majid the same question just two months ago. In an instant she is back in that room with him, a shaft of sunlight falling on the table between them.

'Make me believe you. Prove you've put extremism behind you.'

Majid laughed.

'Define extremism.'

This irritated Kate. This far into their relationship, they didn't even have a common vocabulary. She needed to close the gap.

'Slaughtering innocent people to impose a reign of terror. Making videos of cold-blooded murder . . . Do you want me to go on?'

Majid leaned forward.

'Drones, Daisy Cutter bombs, non-existent weapons of mass destruction . . . Do I need to go on?'

'Is this how you prove yourself to me? You talk the language of the jihadis?'

Majid wasn't fazed by her raised voice.

'I'm talking the language of truth, Kate Armstrong. Have you forgotten what happened in 2003? Two million people marched against the Iraq war. The British government spat in the face of popular opinion and bombed the country anyway. And you expect me to believe in democracy?'

Kate wasn't impressed.

'And how old were you in 2003, Majid? Nine? Ten?'

'The point is,' he insisted, 'that there was a time when the majority of the British people used – what did you call it – the

language of the jihadis. The West's atrocities paved the way for Islamic State.'

'Wrong. Political Islam existed long before the war on terror.'

'And the Crusades, racism, colonialism: how old are they, Kate?'

She threw down her pen in exasperation.

'Save me the history lesson.'

Majid sat back and folded his arms.

'And you save me the sanctimonious hypocrisy.'

She felt she was losing him.

'Bashir Mirza did a good job indoctrinating you.'

'Reminding you how the world works isn't indoctrination. I wasn't brainwashed. I made my own decisions . . .'

Majid trailed off suddenly, remembering why he was here. Kate took advantage of the silence.

'You're not convincing me of your reliability, you know.'

Majid nodded briefly. 'Do you know why you can trust me? Bashir got me to Syria by telling me what I could do for my Muslim brothers and sisters.'

He raised his hands and turned them slowly.

'These hands were meant to heal. I met somebody who showed me how precious life is.'

'Who?'

'It doesn't matter. Not any more.'

Kate made a note. Find out who Majid met. It might be important.

He started talking again.

'Do you know what they expected me to do once I got there? They pushed a gun in my hands. They wanted me to kill those same brothers and sisters in cold blood. It might not sound much to you, but that changed everything for me.'

Kate relives that moment, not just the words, but the conviction with which it was delivered, the bitterness, the sadness in his eyes. The images fade and she is back in Thames House, answering her boss.

'It's a risk, Jen, but I believe it's one worth taking. You're right. We know the main players, at least some of them. We don't know the target. We don't know where the weapons are. Move now and we lop off a few branches. Get our timing right and we tear up the whole tree.'

Jen nods. 'One last thing, his codename. I've always wondered. Why Bungee?'

Kate smiles.

'He fell a long way, but he bounced back up.'

THE PAST

SPRING, 2014

The hospital wasn't what Majid expected. He walked along a corridor with pockmarked walls, glancing up at the flaking, whitewashed ceiling. A strip-light was missing. Everywhere he looked, there was dust. A hot wind blew through windows without panes.

'Not quite the NHS, is it? We try to clean, but the dust keeps coming back. It's the bombing. It covers everything with this dust.'

He turned to see a doctor in her late twenties. Shaima was beautiful, with almond eyes and dark hair, tied in a bun. She went uncovered, something that surprised Majid. He had believed all the women here donned the niqab.

'Did you work in the UK?' he asked. 'Your English is great.'

'I studied there,' she answered. 'Five years. My big brother still lives in London.'

They stepped into a ward that was as bare as it was shabby. Majid saw a little girl lying on a bed with her mother by her side. Both her legs had been amputated. The stumps were wrapped in bandages.

They walked from bed to bed and exchanged words with people torn apart by war; at least, Shaima did. She had to translate for Majid's benefit. They reached a woman in late middle age. Her eyes were those of somebody older.

'This is Noura,' she told him. 'The army came to her village. They tortured her son and burned him alive.'

Majid nodded. 'It is stories like hers that made me come to Syria.'

Noura said something.

'What was that?'

'He was barely more than a boy: seventeen. You remind her of him.'

Majid didn't know what to say.

'Tell her . . . tell her I am sorry for her pain.'

Shaima spoke, and Noura nodded.

'Shukran.'

Thank you.

Majid met Shaima's look. They made their way outside.

'So you came to heal?'

'That was my idea, yes. I only completed two years of my training.'

'You will learn more in a month here than a year at medical school.' She brushed some of the ever-present dust from her coat. 'You will have to learn quickly.'

Shaima wrapped the white coat around her.

'You came with Yusuf, didn't you?'

'That's right. Why do you ask?'

'I don't see you as friends. He talks like an Islamist. You don't.'

Majid dropped his eyes.

'Why are you really here, Majid?'

He laughed.

'I am starting to wonder that myself. I listened to a man. He seemed to have all the answers.'

'And he talked to you of jihad?'

'That's right. How do you know?'

Shaima laughed.

'You're not the first. You won't be the last.'

Shaima's lips parted then closed as she thought what to say. Finally, she spoke.

'We called this our democratic revolution. It started with such hope. With joy. There were marches that filled the streets and stretched as far as the eye could see.' She faltered. 'Look how they answered the people's call for freedom.'

Before them, there was a scene more like a moonscape than a modern town. There were collapsed buildings, houses that had been pounded to dust, minarets that had bent like a giraffe's neck. There was graffiti on the remaining walls, but it had faded. Shaima read the Arabic script for him.

The Syrian people refuse to be humiliated.

A few metres away there was another slogan.

There is no God save Allah.

She pointed out a flag, rippling in the distance.

'I hear you are with Mahmoud.'

'That's right. He was our guide from the border. Without him . . .'

Majid let his arms fall at his sides.

'Without him,' Shaima said, 'you would have turned back and gone home. There is no shame in admitting you made a mistake. You should leave, Majid. There is nothing for you here except death.'

'I have no home,' Majid told her.

She shook her head.

'Mahmoud is a good man among so many butchers. He will let you go. The rest is up to you.'

Majid picked up a stone and threw it.

'What's going to happen: to the war, I mean?'

'It has lasted three years. It could last three more. There is something strange going on, Majid. The people are ground between the army and the jihadis like grain between millstones.'

'The jihadis have more money, more vehicles, more weapons.

Men like Mahmoud will have little choice but to join them or die.'

'How do you still manage to smile?'

Shaima thought for a moment.

'I remember when I was happy. I had such a blissful childhood. My parents doted on my brother and me. We used to go to Latakia. The beach there is beautiful. My father encouraged us to travel and study overseas. It is because of him that I went to London.' She became serious. 'Come back in the morning and we will get to work. I like the phrase in English: good to have you on board.'

Her face brightened. Majid returned her smile and made his way across the rubble-strewn ground to where he was going to meet Yusuf. He was looking forward to seeing Shaima again.

THE PRESENT

22

MONDAY, 4TH JULY

The interview takes place in the head teacher's office. Present on one side of the conference room table, with their backs to the window, are Mr Lucas, Amir's mentor, Mr Khan, and a plainclothes police officer who introduces himself as DI McEvoy. Facing them are Amir and his parents. They find themselves squinting because of the bright sunlight. There are photos on the wall showing the smiling faces of six recent students who won places at Oxford or Cambridge. The message is simple: this is what success looks like. Amir didn't expect to be this nervous, but his heart is slamming.

'I must say, Mr and Mrs Sarwar,' Mr Lucas is saying, 'that I am disappointed you did not inform us of your family's . . .' He takes a minute to select the word. 'Your family's history.'

Dad is about to say something when he registers his wife's warning glance.

'That said, we must look forward. As yet, the press has not picked up on Amir's relationship to your older son. Amir is just a young man who let himself down.'

'DI McEvoy tells me that there is no evidence that you have undergone radicalisation, Amir, but we are concerned about your political trajectory. The police are concerned that you are showing negative and hostile feelings towards the values of this country.'

'I went on a march, that's all.'

His mother leans forward.

'Against our instructions, Mr Lucas.'

Mr Lucas undoes the middle button of his jacket.

'I understand that, Mrs Sarwar. We can't always hold the parents accountable for the actions of their children.' He glances at Amir. 'No matter how irresponsible they may be. As a school, we do have responsibilities, and one of those is to counter extremism. Your elder son—'

'Majid. His name was Majid.'

'Majid took a wrong turn. He was involved with some very dangerous people.'

'You are clearly an intelligent young man, Amir. You must be aware of the issues here.'

Amir starts to say something, but Mr McEvoy talks over his voice and he falls silent.

'We will have to monitor Amir's behaviour in school. Mr Lucas says he will be meeting Mr Khan regularly to review his progress.'

'Progress?' Dad is confused. 'Do you mean his academic work?'

'Mr Lucas is talking about Amir's attitude to integration,' replies McEvoy.

'What does that mean? He is British. He was born in London.'

'Mr Sarwar, without judging you in any way, your elder son . . .' He stops, remembering the plea to refer to him by name. 'Majid died fighting in Syria. Our records show that he had a close relationship with known radicals. You must understand our concern that Amir may be tempted to move in the same circles.'

That draws an instant response from the Sarwars.

'We moved house three times to make sure that did not happen.'

97

There is a short silence during which the tick of the clock seems to echo like a hammer striking metal. Mr Lucas picks up the thread.

'Mr and Mrs Sarwar, we want to do the best by Amir. I have spoken to his form teacher and she tells me that he is a quiet, hardworking boy. I am not accusing Amir of anything—'

Amir interrupts.

'So why do I have to meet Mr Khan? Why are the police here?'

'We want you to take part in the Prevent programme, because it is in your own interests. It is about understanding our British value systems.'

Dad raises an eyebrow.

Mr Lucas clarifies.

'I mean our common values, Mr Sarwar. As you said, we are all proud to be British.'

Amir snorts.

His mother puts her hand on his in an attempt to calm him down.

'Mr Lucas, will this have to go on his school record?'

'Mr Khan will draw up a report on his meetings with Amir. His involvement in the strategy will not appear in any references we write when he applies for jobs or for university. You can be reassured of that.'

'Do we have any choice in the matter?'

DI McEvoy fields this question.

'We would strongly advise that you agree to Amir's participation.'

'So that's it?'

McEvoy clears his throat then gives his answer.

'That's it.'

23

Majid is sitting against the wall of the flat. He picks up his phone and inserts the SIM Kate gave him. He is due to call her. He has barely slept. Bashir's words keep buzzing in his head. The next time he comes, they will go to war. He feels as if he has been searching for a home for a long time. He didn't find it on the streets of London. It wasn't there on the hillsides of Syria or in its broken towns and villages. He relives one of his interviews with Kate.

'I don't know if I can do this.'

'You said you had seen enough innocent people get killed.'

'I know. It's just . . .'

Omar wanted him to be strong, a lion. Majid remembered the day three men surrendered. They were his age. They shared the same hatred of the West. Yet here they were with terror in their eyes, waiting for a man they once thought of as a brother to take their lives. Majid tries to speak a second time. Kate isn't listening.

'Just hear me out. You want a middle way? There isn't one. If you cooperate with us, maybe you can avoid jail-time. If you don't, the going rate is at least four years, more likely ten to twelve with the evidence we have on you. With time off for good behaviour, you might be out by the time you're thirty. That's the price of your caliphate.'

The room where Kate conducted her interviews was bare like this one. He gets to his feet and paces the floor. For a short time after he crossed the border into Turkey, everything was clear. Bashir had to be stopped. Now, nothing is simple. He is thinking of walking straight out of the door and surrendering himself to the waiting surveillance team. That's when his phone goes. It's Kate. He laughs in spite of himself.

'Why didn't you call in? Is everything all right?'

He stares at the time on his phone. 'Am I late?'

'Yes. You were supposed to call in half an hour ago. You've got me worried.'

'I'm OK. Sorry, I lost track of time.'

'Listen, Majid, we have got to keep this brief. If Bashir calls and you don't answer, he will be suspicious. It's Tuesday tomorrow. This is too close for comfort. You're going to have to press him for information. How do you feel about that?'

'I won't let you down.'

THE PAST

SPRING, 2014

The sky was clear and blue. There was the rolling thunder of shelling somewhere across the hills. Majid flinched whenever there was the crash of a missile or the roar of a barrel bomb. The reaction of those around him was different, a kind of weary acceptance. Then there was an ear-splitting explosion. Shaima gave him a reassuring smile.

'Keep working.'

He was helping suture a wound. Tyres crunched on the rubble and shadows flickered across the window. The door burst open and three men rushed in, carrying a child. She was limp, like a doll, smeared with fresh blood that spilled over her skin and clothing. Shaima guided the group to a trolley and helped them lay her down. The child was convulsing. The men stepped back. Shaima was examining the open wound in the girl's leg.

'I think the wound is clean.' She nodded. 'Majid. Apply some pressure.'

They worked quickly, intensely. Once the bleeding stopped, Shaima stepped back. A short man with anxious eyes took her hands. Then he moved on to Majid.

'Shukran, shukran.'

Majid cursed his lack of Arabic and simply nodded. There was no time to talk. Already, another victim of the shelling was being carried in.

'Is it always like this?' Majid asked.

Shaima pulled a face.

'Often, it is worse.'

THE PRESENT

24

MONDAY, 4TH JULY

Majid's phone buzzes in his pocket. He pulls it out and presses it to his ear. On this handset there is only one caller.

'Shoot.'

It is Bashir.

'Go down to the first floor. Not ground. Got me? First floor. Take the stairs, not the lift. Wait there. Just say yes to acknowledge.'

'Yes.'

Majid hangs up. His chest is tight with anxiety. He changes SIMs and calls Kate.

'Something's happening. Bashir wants me to go to the first floor. Tell your people to hurry.'

'We're on to it. You're in luck. The surveillance team just rang in. Bashir is in his car out front. The instant he makes a move, they will track him. Go straight down.'

Majid kills the call, lets himself out of the flat and jogs down the fourteen flights of stairs. His throat is tight. He has no sooner stepped on to the first floor landing than a man detaches himself from the shadows. Majid doesn't recognise him.

'Who are you? Where's Bashir?'

The man is painfully thin, white and blue-eyed. He is wearing a plain black ski hat, which seems odd given the clammy, summer weather.

'No questions. Follow me.'

He leads the way to a service door marked *private*. Majid notices that there are splinters around the lock.

'One you did earlier?'

'Just cut the chat.'

OK, so he doesn't want to be friendly. They walk through an untidy storeroom to another flight of stairs. At the foot of them there is a door that opens on to a small yard, separated from the tenants' car park by a breeze-block wall. Ski Hat gestures Majid forward.

'Over there.'

They are in a side street. Majid searches for some sign of Kate's team. He hopes they are watching from a distance. Ski Hat pulls out a key fob and sidelights flash. Majid commits the blue Escort to memory, just as he did Bashir's plate.

'Where are we going?' Majid demands. 'What happened to Bashir?'

Ski Hat opens the car door.

'You ask too many questions. Bashir does the explanations.'

Majid's throat is dry. If the team has eyes on Bashir then nobody is watching him. Ski Hat drives through dark streets for about half an hour and pulls up. He points out an illuminated window.

'This is it.'

Majid follows Ski Hat to a flat at the end of the block. The property next door is empty, as demonstrated by the steel security grilles on the door and windows. Majid gives the area the once-over.

'Nice.'

Ski Hat's pale blue eyes give him a look that is bordering on contempt. He opens the door on to a room where two Asian men are waiting. They greet him like a long-lost friend. The taller of the pair bumps fists with a bewildered Majid.

'So you're the Rocket Man. Salaam. We saw the vid. You survived an air-to-ground missile. That makes you a legend.'

'Yes, respect. You fought on the front line. What was it like?'

Majid touches the side of his face.

'Painful.'

The answer earns him laughter from the Asian men; not from Ski Hat. The guy has the personality of a cucumber.

'I'm Hamid. This is Faisal.'

Majid nods in the direction of Ski Hat.

'And him?'

'Abu Jihad.'

Majid finds it impossible to suppress a laugh.

'You're kidding me, right?'

He inspects the living room with a cursory glance. 'So what's the score here?'

Kate said to force the pace. That was then. Now he is a fish out of water.

'Bashir will explain when he gets here.'

'Where's the bathroom?'

Hamid points across the hall. Once inside the bathroom, Majid swaps SIMs and texts Kate what he knows. He is about to change the SIMs back when a fist bangs on the door. It's Ski Hat. Majid can't grace him with the name Abu Jihad.

'What are you doing in there, writing your will?'

'I'll be out now.'

'Bashir's just arrived. He says he needs your phone.'

Majid's heart slams. Bashir sounds suspicious. Majid pauses to control his breathing then he remembers something. He adds Ski Hat's number plate to Kate's text and presses send. That done, he swaps the SIMs and looks at the one Kate gave him.

If Bashir does have doubts, this could expose me, he thinks. Reluctantly, he snaps the small, black card and flicks the fragments out of the bathroom window. He takes another moment to compose himself and unlocks the door.

He feels the loss of the SIM keenly.

It was his last link to Five.

Kate is on her way to the block of flats with Jack.

'What a cock-up!' She is playing nervously with her wedding ring. 'The guys on the ground were too slow to respond. I knew something was wrong when Majid said they were sending him to the first floor, not ground level.'

She pounds her fist on the dashboard and Jack shakes his head.

'At least we've got Bungee's text. That was quick thinking.'

She reviews the information Majid was able to send.

'A white male driving a Blue Escort. Calls himself Abu Jihad. Two Asian males, Hamid and Faisal. A maisonette flat within twenty to thirty minutes' drive of the safe house.'

'Any news on the registration number?'

'Nabil is running a check.' She is still playing with her ring. 'We should have known something was going down when Bashir stayed in the car.'

'There's no point beating yourself up over it, Kate. Bashir's clever.'

Kate shakes her head.

'We should be cleverer.' She points. 'We're here. Pull over behind the white van. That's the A4 team.'

She unbuckles her belt and marches over to the two guys in the van.

'OK,' she says, 'who's going to walk me through it?'

The volunteer is a man called Dave Latham, ex-military, experienced, meticulous, ready to go the extra mile. *If Bashir got one over on Latham, he has got to be good.* Latham leads Kate round the corner.

'Bashir was sitting in the car for a good ten minutes before we got your call. Suddenly, he took off at high speed. You could say we were caught between a rock and a hard place. Phil took a walk round the back of the flats while I went to the street corner. All Bashir did was drive round here, abandon the car and take off. I don't know where he went. It's like chasing a ghost.'

'So in a couple of minutes we lost both Bashir and Bungee?' Latham nods.

'That's about the size of it. Sorry, Kate.'

She feels defeated.

'Show me how they did it.'

They climb to the first floor. Latham leads the way through the service door and down to the rear exit.

'Whoever was waiting for Bungee must have parked out here somewhere.'

Kate imagines the sequence of events for a few moments, sighs and pats Latham on the arm.

'Let's put it down to experience. We should have had somebody round the back.'

'So we underestimated Bashir?'

Kate drops her old chewing gum into a dumpster and pops in a new stick.

'That's about the size of it. He let us think we had everything under control then, *bang*, he sprang his surprise.'

She meets Jack by the car and reviews what they have.

'Hamid and Faisal. Mm. That's two pretty generic Muslim names. I doubt whether the computer will turn much up on them. Abu Jihad? A vanilla jihadi. Sounds a better bet.

He may have come up on the radar in the recent past.'

Her phone goes.

'Yes?'

Jack sees the look of disappointment.

'No go on the registration number?'

Kate shakes her head.

'Looks like a cloned plate.'

Jack drums his fingers on the roof of the car.

'You know what this means? Bashir Mirza, Abu Rashid, Jamil Daud. That's cell one. Hamid, Faisal, Abu Jihad. That looks like cell two. Our job just became more complicated.'

They are still talking when Kate's phone goes again. She answers, puts her hand over it and mouths a name.

Jen.

26

Abu Rashid and Jamil Daud are on the move. Under cover of darkness, they slip out of the back door and make their way through the woods to a narrow country lane where Abu Rashid has left his car. They drive to Knebworth station and catch the train into London.

In less than two hours they are walking through the door of the maisonette. Abu Rashid announces their arrival.

'I've brought somebody to meet you, Jamil. He says he's an old friend.'

Jamil seems bewildered. 'What are you talking about?'

Then he sees who is sitting in a worn armchair in the corner of the room.

'Majid! What the . . .?'

Majid laughs.

'What's a little death between friends?'

The two men embrace. Jamil has tears in his eyes. Majid's familiar voice echoes around the room.

'So you didn't forget me then?'

'How can you even ask? It's good to see you, bruv.'

Jamil stammers out a reaction.

'You're alive. How? I saw that video. It was on YouTube until they got it taken down. Everybody was dead. Everybody. I mean, how did you survive something like that?'

'Allah spared me. I was standing over the prisoners, then *boom*. I came to twenty metres away with my face half burned off.'

'Yes, I can see. So you got your battle scar. Does it hurt?'

'Only when I laugh.'

'Seriously.'

'I get some discomfort on this side of my face. Other than that, I've fully recovered.'

Jamil is babbling with excitement.

'You were spared for a purpose. Where's your phone, Abu Rashid? Show him the gun.'

Majid's eyes drift from Jamil to the other guy.

'Gun?'

So, not explosives. This is new. Abu Rashid shows him the picture of the gun. He is enjoying the attention when the feel of the phone in his hand reminds him of something he has to do.

'Phone,' he says. 'I need the phone back, Majid – Bashir's instructions.'

Majid hands it over.

'What's the matter? Don't you guys trust me?'

'Of course we trust you, brother. You're the Rocket Man. But it's the same rule for everybody. Strictly radio silence from now on. Three days. Got that? Three days.'

He turns to the group.

'The Kuffs say never again. What do we say, mujahideen?'

Fists punch the air and they chant. Majid chants as loudly and eagerly as everybody else.

'Again, again, *again*.'

THE PRESENT

27

TUESDAY, 5TH JULY

'We've screwed up. We've screwed up big time. First the London safe house, now bloody Hertfordshire. Everybody we've been watching is on the move and we don't know where. The word "surveillance" is in *A4 surveillance team* for a reason.'

Jack Cole frowns for Kate to keep her voice down.

'What's the time, Jack?'

He glances at his watch.

'Twelve seventeen.'

'The CTC meeting started at nine. Jen said she would be back by half past eleven. I don't like this.'

Jack is on edge himself. The CTC is the Counter-Terrorist Committee, established in the immediate aftermath of nine/eleven. It comprises the Home Office, the Metropolitan Police, the signals intelligence centre, GCHQ and the security services MI5 and MI6.

'We've got two terrorist cells on the loose and nobody knows where the hell either of them are. This is a foul-up of titanic proportions. Either Bashir Mirza is a very lucky man or a tactical genius. Neither option gives me much comfort.'

Kate stares at the large screen at the front of the briefing room in the heart of Thames House.

Regnum Defende.

Defend the Realm.

We have to succeed every time.
They only have to succeed once.

At that moment stiletto heels click in the corridor outside and Jen Sherbourne walks in alone. She proceeds straight to the front of the room and slots a memory stick into the laptop. A new menu replaces the MI5 crest. There are no formalities.

'You may know that I have come here straight from the CTC. It would be an understatement to say that the Minister is angry. The word "ballistic" might sum it up more accurately. The service is in the spotlight.'

She uses her clicker to bring up a series of slides.

'This is Jamil Daud, twenty-one years old. Not the brightest blade of grass in the lawn, according to his school reports, but a convinced jihadi.'

Second slide.

'This is David Obi, a twenty-eight-year-old man of Nigerian descent from East London. He has no criminal convictions and seems to have been radicalised while at university. Acquaintances have testified to his cold, impersonal nature. He goes by the name Abu Rashid.'

Jen trains her ice-cold eyes on her audience then brings up the next slide.

'For those of you unfamiliar with him, this is Bungee – aka Majid Sarwar, twenty-one years old. Bungee is Kate's agent. We have lost contact with him. We assume Bashir Mirza is preventing the use of mobile phones as they prepare their attack on the seven/seven commemoration.'

Next slide.

'There is some cause for caution, however. This is Majid Sarwar's younger brother, Amir, sixteen years old. Amir was arrested during a demonstration outside a London mosque on Saturday.'

A murmur goes round the room.

'The police have made a referral under Prevent's Channel

scheme. It is only a matter of time before the media makes the connection with Bungee.'

A man at the back of the room raises his hand.

'Let me get this straight. One brother goes to fight in Syria. The other comes up on the radar here. That is two extremists in the same family. On what grounds are we trusting Bungee?'

Jen hears him out.

'We have no evidence that Amir has been radicalised. For the time being, we will proceed on the assumption that Bungee is our asset, but we must be prepared to act on the alternative explanation for this period of silence. He gave us information. It could all be false.'

Next slide.

'This is what we know about the alleged second cell. We have three names: Hamid, Faisal and Abu Jihad.'

'As yet, we have no more information.'

She takes a breath.

Next slide.

'Last but not least, meet our ringleader, Bashir Mirza.'

Bashir's name gets a reaction.

'He is thirty years old. He actively groomed Majid Sarwar and Jamil Daud. We believe Bashir to be extremely dangerous. He has a string of convictions for drug offences and violence, including putting a police officer in hospital for six weeks.

'Bashir Mirza is intelligent and ruthless. He has had contact with Turkish drug gangs in the past. He seems to have learned his logistical skills from them. Are there any questions?'

'What are their targets?'

Next slide.

'You are all familiar with the images of July seventh, 2005. Bashir Mirza seems to want to enact a repeat. It would be the most extreme provocation ever carried out on British soil.'

Next slide.

The image provokes another hum of apprehension around the room.

'We fear that the attack on the commemoration may only be phase one of a more sophisticated plan. Many of you will recognise the Manchester Central Convention Centre, built on the site of the old Manchester Central Railway Station. It is here that the Home Secretary will address the Anti-terrorist Alliance Conference on Saturday afternoon.'

She lets the details sink in. 'Here's the bottom line, people. We have lost track of two dangerous cells. They may be planning not one, but two spectaculars: in other words, a coordinated multi-target assault. We have to find them and put them out of action.'

She removes the memory stick and heads for the door.

'Let's get to work.'

28

Karen Morgan has just made a connection. She is ambitious and intelligent and she may just have stumbled across the story that will secure her a move up from the local paper on which she has worked for six months to the nationals. It is the name of the boy arrested at the England Awakes march.

Sarwar.

Amir Sarwar.

The moment she read the copy from her colleague, she could feel her skin tingle with anticipation. Her last job was on another small local rag, six miles across the city. Their biggest story was about a local guy, a medical student, who took off to Syria and died fighting for the Islamic State. She has followed a digital trail and it has led her from a mouthy sixteen-year-old on a demonstration to a much bigger fish.

She murmurs a name to herself and makes a call.

'Mark? Hi, it's Karen. Yes, I'm good. I know, long time no see.' Mark used to fancy her rotten and he is obviously hoping this phone call is pleasure, not business. 'Anyhow, can I pick your brains about something?'

She hears the disappointment in his voice. A short phone conversation tells her everything she needs to know. She spends the next half-hour checking and double-checking. With each confirmation, her pulse rate quickens.

'Gotcha!'

Five minutes later, she is sitting across the desk from her editor, Tom Carrick.

'So what have you got, Karen? What makes Amir Sarwar so important?'

'He isn't important in himself, Tom, but I found an article from last year. It's about his brother.'

Karen reads out loud:

'*Two British citizens have died fighting for Syrian rebels linked to Islamic State, amid fears that the country's civil war is radicalising young people in the United Kingdom.*'

Tom stares at Karen and starts to laugh.

'You and your sixth sense, eh?'

She reads on:

'*Two of the Britons, both from London, were killed in a rocket attack near Raqaa, an Islamic State stronghold. They were among a dozen British extremists fighting for the rebel group, also known as ISIL or Daesh. The men are named as Yusuf Al-Suri and . . . Majid Sarwar, both twenty.*'

'You're quite sure this Majid Sarwar is Amir's brother?'

'They're brothers all right.' She hands him a print-off. 'Same address. Here's a family photo.' She is enjoying watching Tom's reaction. Two more printed sheets land on his desk. 'Here is corroboration.'

Tom examines everything carefully.

There is no mistake.

29

Majid feels somebody kicking his bare foot and opens his eyes. Bashir is grinning down at him.

'I hope you slept well.'

'This sofa wasn't built for a six-footer,' Majid grumbles.

Abu Rashid is asleep in the armchair opposite.

'He could sleep on a washing line. There is as much life in him as a sack of rice,' says Bashir, delivering the same non-too-subtle wake-up call to Abu Rashid. Then he rouses Jamil, who is curled up in a sleeping bag on the floor.

'We've got to go. Now.'

Faisal has just walked in the room, rubbing the sleep from his eyes like a little boy.

'Where are we going?'

Bashir scowls.

'You know better than to ask.'

Majid's mind is racing. There are two days to go. If he does what Bashir says, countless people will die. He has to push it.

'That's not good enough, Bashir.'

The shock around the room is so heavy he could touch it.

'What did you say?'

'We're not kids. Either you let the rest of us in on this plan of yours or I walk. Warriors fight best when they understand their mission.'

Bashir's eyes blaze with indignation.

'What gives you the right to question me, Majid?'

He is aware of Abu Rashid, Jamil and Faisal watching. *OK, Kate, this is me pushing it.*

'What about a year on the battlefield, months recovering from my injuries? How long did you spend on the front line, *my brother?*'

Majid's neck is burning. Has he overdone it? Bashir's gaze roves round the room. Everybody is waiting to see how he reacts to this challenge to his authority. He reaches into his pocket and Majid's nerves melt. To his relief, Bashir laughs out loud and slaps him on the shoulder. Majid sees what Bashir has taken from his pocket. He is gripping his phone.

'Do you see? This is what jihad does to a man. I sent a boy to war. He returned a mujahid.'

Majid rejects the crude attempt at flattery.

'The plan, Bashir. You're asking us to be martyrs, but you don't give us respect. What's the plan?'

Faisal is the one who speaks.

'In two days we surrender our lives to Allah: me, Hamid, Abu Jihad. Does that answer your question?'

'Just you three?'

'Just us.'

Majid turns shocked eyes on Bashir.

'And the rest of us?'

'The commemoration is only stage one, Majid. Remember this?'

He mimics the sound of an automatic rifle. Jamil frowns.

'I don't get it.'

Faisal shakes his head and goes to a cupboard.

'Is this enough explanation for you?'

He is holding a suicide vest. Majid's flesh crawls. Bashir rests a hand on Faisal's shoulder.

'Stage one. The bomber.'

He walks to Majid and forces the phone in front of his face. 'Stage two. The shooter. This is why we wanted you. You've got experience on the battlefield. You're the main man.'

Experience on the battlefield? Yusuf forced a gun into his hands, got him to train, got him to fight. Majid stares at the image then hands the phone back.

Majid is back on an exposed hillside just a few miles from Raqaa, standing over the three Al Nusra fighters. First you fight side by side. Then Omar tells you to put a bullet in the back of each man's head. This is their jihad.

You become the executioner of your own brothers.

30

Majid has the address. Now he needs a phone. Bashir isn't going to make it easy. When Majid went to brush his teeth, Bashir told him to leave the door open. 'Just precautions.' He said it with a wink that gave Majid no comfort.

They walk to the tube, each of the four men keeping an eye on the other three. They travel two stops and pick up Bashir's latest vehicle from a private car park. There is no opportunity to get a message to Kate. Now they are driving north. All the signs are for the M1.

Time to press it again. Majid stretches, trying to look casual.

'We still haven't eaten,' he reminds Bashir.

They pull over at a fried chicken restaurant called Chik Chik Chicken. Majid cracks a joke.

'I hear this one's got a Michelin star.'

There are only six tables. Most of the trade is in takeaways. *There has to be a way to contact Kate, let her know what's going down.* He sees a man going through the back door. Bashir is at the counter, ordering the food. Majid sees his chance.

'I need to take a leak.'

Jamil is staring out of the window. Abu Rashid shrugs.

'You don't need my permission.'

Majid crosses to the door, hoping Bashir hasn't noticed. There is another man, washing his hands. Majid has to be quick. The instant Bashir sees he's gone, he will be in here like a flash.

'Excuse me,' Majid says. 'Can I ask a favour?'

The man, a black guy in his thirties, looks at him with a certain amount of suspicion.

'I need to make a call. Could I borrow your phone? Thirty seconds max. I'll pay for it.' Remembering Jamil, he adds, 'It's my mum. She's got cancer.'

The man's features relax.

'Why didn't you say so?' He hands over his phone. 'Take as long as you like.'

Majid rings Kate's number, the one she told him to memorise in case of emergencies. She picks up on the third ring.

'Where are you?'

Majid's eyes are on the door. His throat is tight with anxiety.

'Chicken joint. Look, I don't have long. The first cell is going to hit the commemoration. They are at this address.'

There is silence while Kate makes a note. Majid can't take his eyes off the door.

'What about you?'

'He's got something else planned for us. No details yet.'

'Where's he taking you? Any clues?'

He sees the phone's owner staring and rushes out an answer.

'North, I think. I've got to go.'

He kills the call and hands the phone back.

'Your mum, you say?' the guy grunts. 'That isn't how I talk to mine.'

He walks out, clearly angry. Bashir comes through the open door.

'What are you doing here, Majid? You've been a while.'

'What, are you timing me now?'

Majid sounds tough, but he wants to throw up. He washes his hands, fighting the shake in his fingers. His legs are like jelly. Bashir considers him for a moment.

'Your food is on the table. We don't have long.'
Majid knows what he's got to do.
Breathe. Steady yourself. See this thing through.

THE PRESENT

31

WEDNESDAY, 6TH JULY

Kate is sitting in a transit van with Jack in tow, listening to the crackle of radio traffic. Earlier, Special Branch inserted a fibre-optic cable into an airbrick so that they can monitor the movements of the occupants in the London maisonette. They now have footage of the second cell. The three men look bored and listless. The only sign that they could be preparing an act of terrorism is a blanket-covered bump in the middle of the living room floor. Jack leans forward, examining the screen.

There is more radio chatter. This time it is the firearms team leader. The Met has deployed its specialist firearms command, SCO19, also known as Trojans because of their armed response vehicles. The armed officers are ready to go in.

'Confirmed: three males; two Asian, one white. No other occupants. We have no visual of bomb-making equipment, no visible firearms. Are you getting audio and video feed?'

'Confirm that.'

There is a short pause.

'The only object of interest is whatever the blanket is covering.'

Kate rubs her palms on her skirt. Her job is done. The house is identified. The firearms unit takes responsibility for the raid.

'Three targets. One unidentified object.'

The radio crackles again and the image on the screen jerks, breaking up slightly.

'Ready for the assault. On my count.'

Kate is jumpy. One misjudgement will lead to disaster.

'I wish this was over.'

'It won't be long now,' Jack Cole answers.

There is a final message from the firearms team leader.

'Thirty seconds away. Twenty.'

In her mind's eye, Kate can see the assault team assembling in silence, the Glock 17s strapped to their thighs. When the order comes to go in, it is like a whipcrack.

'Go, go, go!'

There is a crash as the Enforcer door-ram breaches the lock. Dark-garbed figures fill the screen, firearms trained on the startled occupants. There is no resistance, no attempt to reach the blanket. The suddenness of the operation has paralysed them, choked off any impulse to resist. Soon the three men are biting the carpet, arms restrained behind their backs. A second team is rushing an object away for examination; it looks like a bag. It is some time before a fist pounds on the van door and Jack opens up. There is an exchange of conversation and he turns to Kate.

'The house is secured. We're clear to approach.'

Groups of local residents are watching the forensic team going into the house. Kate watches them: mothers, fathers, grandparents, children. She imagines what the cell could do to them. They sum up the vulnerability of human life.

'What was under the blanket?'

One of the firearms officers holds the front door open.

'See for yourself.'

'Suicide vest. They hadn't got round to arming it. No automatic weapons?'

'No, no shooters.'

'What's in the bag?'

'Improvised device. Explosives. Ball bearings. Nails. Nasty. Designed to cause the maximum injury. Your intel was spot on, Kate. Job done.'

Kate doesn't comment.

On the way back to Thames House, there is no discussion of what happened. They are focused on stage two of the operation. Jack is the first to share his thoughts.

'Well, we took out cell one with a day to go. Now we've got four days to stop cell two.'

'So you're sure the target is the anti-terrorism conference?'

'It's the obvious candidate.'

'All I'm saying is, we can't exclude other possibilities. I still think London is favourite. Did you compile the list of targets?'

'You know I did.'

Kate's ringtone breaks the tension. It's Nabil. She listens, acknowledges his message and hangs up.

'Something wrong?' Jack asks.

'Nabil just identified one of the men Abu Rashid met. His name is Radek Kalas, a known gunrunner from the Czech Republic.'

Jack grimaces.

'Looks like we're not out of the woods yet.'

32

Nasima is fiddling with her bag's dodgy zip and chatting to Lucy when she sees a familiar figure standing on the far pavement.

'What's Dad doing here?'

Amir stops wrestling around with Nikel and follows the direction of Nasima's stare. Already, a sense of unease is ticking away inside him.

'Now he's waving.' Rolled eyes follow. 'What have I done wrong this time?'

Nasima sighs. 'It isn't always about you, Amir. If he has taken time off work, it must be serious.'

Lucy sees them starting to walk away.

'Are you two going somewhere?' she asks. 'I thought you were coming round to mine later, Nas.'

Nasima shoulders her school bag.

'Looks like there might be a change of plan, Luce. Dad hasn't picked us up from school since we were in juniors.' She sees the expression on her father's face. The flickering anxiety is new and unsettling. 'I'll call you, OK?'

Lucy is left standing with Nikel, wondering what's going on. Already, Nasima has forgotten about her.

'Dad looks really worried. What's going on?'

Their father is hurrying across the busy road. For a moment he is stranded between two lanes of traffic, hopping from one foot to the other as he looks for a gap. Finally, he reaches the pavement.

'We have to go.'

His voice is urgent. He has his eyes on the pedestrians as they hurry by. Nasima's voice is shaky.

'Dad, are you all right? What's wrong?'

He shakes his head.

'Not here, Nasima. Follow me. We've got to go.'

The twins are aware of Nikel and Lucy staring as they weave their way across the road to the family car.

'Dad, why are you behaving like this?'

'Keep going. I will explain in the car.'

By now, Amir is becoming as agitated as his sister. He slips into the passenger seat and Nasima climbs into the back.

'Is this about me?'

There is no answer. Dad is driving fast.

'Dad,' Amir murmurs, 'I think you need to slow down.'

Then a yell of warning. 'Dad!'

A woman stops dead on a zebra crossing as Dad slams on the brakes. The car rocks on its suspension and Dad seems to crumple before his children. The pedestrian glares at him then carries on her way. Nasima and Amir watch their father resting his head on the steering wheel until the driver behind hits his horn. Dad clears the shock from his mind and drives on.

'I wasn't concentrating. No more questions until we get to the hotel.'

Amir turns to look at Nasima. Hotel?

She shrugs her bewilderment.

The drive takes fifteen minutes. The hotel is part of a no-frills, cut-price chain. Dad pulls into a corner parking bay, unfastens his seatbelt and leads them into the building. He gains access to the stairs with his key card.

'Where's Mum?' Nasima asks.

'She is upstairs.'

They climb the stairs and Dad unlocks the door. Mum rises to her feet. There are two suitcases in the middle of the room and two sports bags belonging to the twins.

'What is this? Where are we going?'

'We are staying right here,' their father says. 'We need to stay away from the flat until things calm down.'

He walks to the window and peers outside.

'Dad, what's wrong? What are you looking for?'

'Reporters. They came round the flat.'

Amir throws his head back.

'Reporters. So it *is* about me.'

'No, Amir,' Mum says. 'It is not about you. It's Majid. The press has made the connection.'

'This is spinning out of control,' Dad says. 'Somehow, journalists at the *Reporter* have found out about Majid. I don't know how they did it, but they have put it all together: Amir's arrest, his referral to Prevent, the fact that Majid joined those takfiris. They are going to publish an article tomorrow. By Friday morning, everybody will know about Majid. We will be a family of extremists.'

'But that's crazy,' Nasima cries. 'Amir isn't Majid. How can they do this to us?'

A few spots of rain strike the windowpane.

'And that's why we're hiding out here?'

'Yes. Your mother and I wanted to protect you from those vultures. The newspapers have got everything. They are going to paint us as terrorists.'

He finds himself speaking to his dead son. 'Oh, Majid, if only you knew what your madness has done to us.'

Nasima takes one of her father's hands between hers.

'What do we do now, Abbu-ji?'

Her father shakes his head.

'I don't know. I honestly don't know.'

Bashir pulls over. They are in a layby on a lonely country road. Majid's heart kicks.

'Why are we stopping here?'

Bashir ignores the question.

'Get out.'

There are woods to their left.

Majid doesn't like the chain of events. 'What's this about?'

Bashir opens the boot.

'Get your bags, all of you.'

Jamil is jumpy.

'What for?'

'Somebody ratted the cell out to the police. I'm going to find out who.'

'I don't understand.'

Bashir held out his phone.

'There was a raid.'

Majid feigns shock.

'How? How the hell did they know where to look?'

Bashir presses his knuckles into his temple.

'That's what I'm trying to find out.'

He draws a butterfly knife.

'Move.'

Before long, they are in a clearing. It is a peaceful spot.

There is birdsong and dappled sunlight, but Majid is uneasy. Bashir starts with Abu Rashid.

'Jamil, pat him down.'

Jamil finds a set of keys, a knife, some change and not much else. It doesn't give Majid any confidence that both Bashir and Abu Rashid are carrying shanks.

'Now check his bag.'

Jamil goes through it with trembling hands.

'Nothing.'

'OK, one down. Now Majid.'

Jamil repeats the operation. At one point he meets Majid's gaze. There is terror in Jamil's eyes. Something is wrong.

Bashir supervises the bag search. Satisfied, he turns to Abu Rashid.

'Now, you search Jamil.'

At this point, Jamil breaks down.

'Look, I've got to tell you something.'

Bashir shakes his head fiercely and points the blade at Jamil's face.

'Not a word or I'll give you a joker's smile.'

Abu Rashid goes through the bag, feels something and tugs at the bag's lining. 'He's got something hidden.'

He holds up a phone. Jamil's eyes widen.

'So who've you been phoning, Jamil? Got friends in the government?'

Majid feels sick.

'It's not the way it looks. I had to hide the phone. My mum's ill. Cancer. I just wanted to check in with my sisters, see she was OK. You can look at my call history.'

Bashir's face doesn't betray any emotion.

'Bashir, I'm telling the truth. Ask Majid. He knows my mum. She hasn't been well.'

Majid stumbles out a confirmation.

'That's right. It was all going on before I left for Syria. She was starting chemo. Come on. Cut him some slack.'

Abu Rashid folds his arms. 'We said no phones. End of. Somebody gave Five the low-down on the house. I think we've found our rat.'

Jamil is in full panic mode. He understands the consequences of the hidden phone.

'Listen. Please. Just listen to me. I know it looks bad, but I can't just forget about my mum. Have some heart.' He looks at Majid. 'You know I'm no plant, Majid. Tell them. Please!'

Majid can feel the pulse throbbing in his throat. This is bad.

'Check his calls, Bashir. I've known this guy since we were kids. I would trust him with my life. He would never work for the security services.'

'That's right.' Jamil is begging with his life. There are sweat stains on his shirt. 'I hate them. If somebody's passing information, it ain't me.'

Bashir is deaf to his pleas.

'There's a mole, Majid. They knew about our guys. Put two and two together, bro.'

Majid feels hope ebbing away. Bashir is standing to one side of Jamil, Abu Rashid to the other.

'Look, let's talk about this.'

'There's no time, Majid. We've got to move. Now.'

Abu Rashid has produced his own knife, a large blade with a serrated edge. Jamil's eyes widen. Now he is trembling, spittle running on to his chin.

'Don't do this, man. I didn't talk to anybody.'

'What's the problem?' Abu Rashid demands. 'You've been talking about martyrdom. It's going to come a little early, that's all.'

Jamil is begging for his life.

'The phone is for my mum. Tell him, Majid. Tell him!'

Abu Rashid is pushing Jamil deeper into the trees. Majid looks on and it is as if he is dreaming. Everything he sees, everything he hears is distant, echoing strangely.

'Help me, Majid. Help me!'

Jamil's cries are like stones dropping into water, sending out ripples of helpless fear, but Majid doesn't move. He looks on, and the horror envelops him like a shroud.

Moments later there is a small, sharp cry and crows rise noisily from the undergrowth.

Abu Rashid reappears.

'Let's go.'

THE PAST

SPRING, 2014

The explosion woke Majid. He had got used to the sights and sounds of war, but there was a sound he would remember in his dreams for the rest of his life: this single crack, followed by an ominous rumble. An hour after the shell hit, he became aware of a figure in the doorway.

'Yusuf? What's wrong?'

'You've got to come. It's the hospital.'

Majid followed Yusuf to the Hilux. He was numb. His footsteps seemed to fall in a different world to this one. The vehicle's engine was throbbing, ready to leave. Soon they were roaring past cypress trees. There were a few poppies nodding in the breeze. They saw the usual sights: the rubble that was once the dome of a mosque, the numerous craters left by the regime's merciless shelling, a cemetery framed in the dawn light. Majid stared numbly at his surroundings. Women passed in fluttering black abayas. Majid barely registered the scene.

He eventually recognised the fig grove to their left. They were nearly there. That's when they saw the smoke on the horizon. As they climbed down from the Hilux, Mahmoud appeared, wearing the black of the Islamic State. Majid rushed towards him.

'Shaima, is she . . .'

'I'm sorry, Majid. The missile brought the roof down on her

while she was sleeping. She wouldn't have felt any pain.'

That is how he learned of her death. While Mahmoud's voice died away, the last survivors to be pulled out of the rubble were staggering into one another, falling against their rescuers. Majid placed his hands on the side of the Hilux and closed his eyes.

'Where is she? I want to see her.'

He found her laid out on a blanket. The sun was on her face. She was covered in dust.

'It is as if she is sleeping.'

Majid's heart was as hard and dead as a stone. He couldn't believe what had happened.

'She was good. She was the best person I ever met.'

Yusuf was by his side.

'I know how you felt about Shaima. Do you want to avenge her?'

A black fire had ignited inside Majid's soul.

'Yes.'

'By force of arms?'

'Yes.'

Yusuf nodded.

'Then I will show you the way.'

THURSDAY, 7TH JULY

Majid feels like a prisoner.

There are two bedrooms in the small terraced house in Dunstable, but Bashir insists that they all sleep in the same room. Majid gazes out at the cramped yard, the retail units just beyond the wall, the scrap of dull sky. The other two never let him out of their sight. He watches the late afternoon light and runs the same questions through his mind. Why here? What is the target? There is still no sign of the guns, just that one tantalising photo.

Majid drops into an armchair that has seen better days. The varnish on the arms is cracked and peeling. There is a spring working its way through the upholstery. He keeps reliving the moment Abu Rashid marched Jamil to his death.

Abu Rashid complains loudly. 'The waiting is killing me.'

Bashir looks at Majid.

'What about you, Rocket Man?'

Majid forces out a reply.

'Yes, I'm bored.'

Bashir grunts.

'You don't have enough to occupy your tiny minds.'

'So give us something to do. Tell us about the target.'

'Why the hurry, Majid? Are you so hungry for martyrdom?'

Majid wonders whether it is time to take risks.

'You say I'm the main man, Bashir. You want me to be your

warrior, but you don't trust me. I thought we'd had this out.'

He has got Abu Rashid's attention. He clearly wants to know how this is going to play with Bashir.

'You owe me, Bashir. I lost a good friend in Syria. I lost another here.'

'Jamil was a rat, Majid. He had a phone hidden in his room.'

This time, Majid is not pushing at the boundaries. He is speaking from the heart. 'You had him killed for nothing, Bashir. That phone was to call his mum. I think you even know that. Why did you kill him? Does it give you some kind of kick?'

He has rattled Bashir's cage. Steely eyes fix him.

'I couldn't take any risks with Jamil. He had a big mouth. I couldn't trust him.'

Majid has confirmed something he half knew already.

'This wasn't about the phone, was it? You just wanted to get rid of him.' He is meant to be a warrior, a mujahid. He has got to play the part: 'If you know a man is a traitor, it's right to kill him. You couldn't be sure about Jamil.'

'Is that right?' Bashir says. 'So if Jamil wasn't the mole, who was?'

Majid knows he has stepped on to dangerous ground. Bashir's suspicion is like a tripwire under his foot. He fights his way back.

'I don't think there is a mole, Bashir. Five had eyes on us. We thought we lost them. Maybe we didn't. You're just playing that card to keep everybody on their toes.'

Abu Rashid laughs.

'He's got you there.'

Bashir continues to examine Majid's face as if seeing him properly for the first time.

'So what's the target?'

Bashir turns away.

'Nice try, but operational decisions stay with me. Five have won one battle. They won't win the next.'

35

There is a new set of CCTV stills on Kate's desk. She also has the entire footage on her laptop. Jen leans forward and peers over Kate's shoulder.

'This is Newport Pagnell Services,' Jack explains. 'First, the East London house, now a positive ID. Our luck is changing.'

The images of the three men are as clear as a bell.

'That seals the deal,' Jen comments. 'It's the Manchester conference.'

Jack seems satisfied with his morning's work. He can't help giving Kate a knowing glance.

'They must be in the city by now. I wish we'd picked up their trail earlier.'

Kate continues to survey the pictures. Jen watches her before speaking.

'You're very quiet, Kate. Have you got something on your mind?'

'I'm not sure.'

'If there's something you think we've missed, you need to say.'

'It's not that we've missed anything. It's just . . . The timings are all wrong. We know they left the East London house by ten. We have a sighting on the Underground an hour later. Then this big gap until they turn up at Newport Pagnell. What were they doing in the meantime?' A slight pause, then: 'You said it yourself. Bashir's clever. He plans. He slips out of sight like that.' She snaps her fingers. 'He lets us watch him when he wants. What if this is another of his tricks? All these images. I mean, it's as if he wanted us to follow his movements.'

'Kate,' Jack answers, 'sometimes you have to accept the obvious. The reason Manchester is staring us in the face is simple. It's the target. Everybody will be at the convention centre: police officers, security personnel, the Home Secretary. How often do our jihadi friends get an opportunity like this?'

Kate feels patronised.

'What are the chances of them getting through, Jack? Bashir may be a rogue, some would say an amateur, but he is a serious operator, possibly the most dangerous activist we have faced since seven/seven. I don't see him launching an attack with next to no chance of success.'

Jen looks thoughtful.

'So if Manchester isn't the target, what is, Kate?'

Kate slumps back in her seat.

'I don't know. I'm still going through the list Jack drew up.'

Jen steps in.

'Analyse it all you like, Kate, but if you want to convince me that the cell has a different target, you need to show me hard evidence.'

Kate shuts her eyes. This is wrong, so wrong. She knows Bashir is playing them. Majid is still out of contact so Bashir must be keeping a close eye on him.

Lives are at stake. A face fills her thoughts. Majid, the man who came back from the dead. *Talk to me, Majid. Tell me what they're planning.*

Suddenly, Majid's eyes are burning through her.

'You don't know what makes me tick, Kate. You can't even begin to imagine.'

I can't even begin to imagine, Kate thinks. *Maybe I can't. I can't walk around in your skin, Majid, but I can understand your motives.*

She returns to the question that is haunting her. *If not Manchester, where? Just get in touch, Majid. Give me a clue.*

Please.

36

Mum deposits a carrier bag on the bed and lays out the *Reporter* for everyone to look at. Amir's verdict is instant.

'They're out to destroy us!'

The paper has gone big on the story: *Jihad Family Sarwar*.

Underneath reads: *Brothers engaged in extremist Islam*. There is the photograph of Amir being arrested. There is a thumbprint photo of Majid as a schoolboy, but the image that dominates the spread is an Islamic State fighter atop a tank, a huge, black flag rippling behind him.

'If you think this is bad, read the editorial.'

Nasima begins with the headline.

'*Islamic extremism must not be allowed to flourish.*' There is the same look on all four faces, one of utter dismay. '*According to the Government's own measure, the likelihood of a terrorist attack in the capital is 'Critical'. We must not be complacent. It is estimated that between 500 and 1,500 UK citizens have chosen to travel to the Middle East to take part in a savage conflict. If they return home, they represent a severe threat to national security.*

'*More worrying still is the possibility that Majid Sarwar's family shares at least some of his poisonous ideology.*'

Nasima puts the paper down.

'Dad, I don't want to read any more. How am I supposed to go back to school after this?'

Her father turns to comfort her.

'There is nothing here that is an outright lie. It is the way everything is presented. We can't have any argument with what they say about Majid. As for the rest, all Amir did was shout at a crowd of racists. Anybody reading it would think that we have been organising a training camp for armed insurrection.'

Mum's face is pinched with anxiety.

Mum remembers Amir.

'Can you imagine what Mr Lucas is going to think?'

A second thought hits her.

'Naveed, what about your job? You have to deal with the public.'

'I tried to prepare my line manager. I didn't expect anything like this. I will have to call her back.'

Nasima's eyes widen as the implications of the article sink in.

'What will my friends say? I've got to talk to Lucy.'

Amir wraps his arms round his head.

'There's no way I can go back.'

37

Jack delivers the message with his usual sense of high drama.

'We're out of here, Kate. Jen's orders.'

Kate has been watching YouTube clips of Bashir Mirza's speeches. The last was made two years ago. There are the usual condemnations of the Zionist-Crusader enemy, but he reserves most of his fury for what the press like to call moderate Muslims. He uses a different vocabulary to the media. They are apostates, false Muslims. That gives her pause for thought. She will return to it later. Right now, she has more pressing business.

'She's come to a decision. It's Manchester.'

Kate is deflated. Jen has dismissed the idea that it could be London. It isn't hard to know why her theory has been sidelined. It is three days since Majid last made contact. She is aware of the muttering. *OK, so he gave us the East London cell. What if it is all just a bit too easy? Offer up a sacrificial lamb to hit the main target.* Kate fiddles with her wedding ring, the way she always does when she is under stress. If anyone had asked her two days ago, even yesterday, whether she trusted Bungee, she would have answered without hesitation. Yes. Absolutely. Now, she just does not know.

'Are you sure about Manchester, Jack? Can you really be a hundred per cent certain? Why dismiss the alternatives? I just don't buy the idea of Bashir moving outside his comfort zone. Everything we know about him suggests otherwise.'

'You just can't accept the obvious, can you?'

She grabs his sleeve.

'Just listen to me! I am not trying to put you down, Jack, if that's what you think. I'm terrified we're putting all our eggs in the wrong basket. What do we know about Bashir Mirza? He is intelligent. He has consistently been one step ahead of us. He is calculating. He plans every detail. All of a sudden, his mug-shot is all over CCTV. Do you really think he suddenly got careless?'

Jack isn't interested in complications.

'You talk as if Bashir is some kind of genius. He was a petty criminal, a violent drug dealer. He's a law unto himself. OK, he's cunning and charismatic, but he's hardly infallible. He's made a mistake. Kate, don't lose a sense of proportion.'

Kate follows Jack outside.

She can't shake the feeling that something is wrong.

THE PRESENT

FRIDAY, 8TH JULY

Bashir has finished shaving his beard and body hair. He wipes the foam from his face and glances at Majid, who is standing at the door.

'Have you got something to say, Majid?'

'You haven't shaved your head. Why not?'

Majid knows the significance of the ritual. They will be cleansed when they enter Heaven. Bashir doesn't expect to survive.

'In good time. We do not want to draw attention to ourselves. The security services are on the lookout for three bearded fighters. Instead, we are clean-shaven, with smart haircuts. We are almost unrecognisable.'

Abu Rashid is lolling in a chair in front of the TV. He has a vanity mirror and he is looking at his reflection.

'You should be a hairdresser, Bashir.'

Bashir doesn't answer. He pulls out his phone and examines the screen then he starts to jingle his car keys in his pocket. Majid knows what this means.

Abu Rashid continues to lounge in front of the TV. His eyelids are growing heavy, his body language relaxed. Majid is willing him to sleep. He has been out of contact with Kate for far too long and the attack is imminent. Majid's hands are clammy at the thought of what is round the corner. He approaches the window and looks out into the street. The car is gone.

'Why don't you sit down, Majid?' yawns Abu Rashid. 'You never stop pacing. I'm trying to sleep here.'

Majid nods and sinks into the other armchair.

Majid remembers the terror in Jamil's eyes. He feels sick. He sucks in a few breaths, runs his hands over his scalp, feeling his new, short hairstyle. Abu Rashid's head is tilted to one side. He can hear Abu Rashid's regular breathing. This is the best chance he is going to get. He edges his way across the room and eases the door open. He puts the door on the snip, waits a second, listening to Abu Rashid's rhythmic breathing and steps on to the pavement.

He shifts his attention to a group of young guys on the pavement opposite. His pulse is throbbing violently.

'Hi, my phone's out of charge . . .'

'So charge it.'

The reply gets a laugh.

'No, you don't understand. I have an urgent call to make.'

He sees the wheels.

'How urgent?'

Majid glances at the house. He produces a five-pound note. 'This urgent.'

The teenagers give him a pitying look.

'Make it a twenty and you're on.'

Majid produces another two fivers and a few coins.

'This is all I have.'

He sees an outstretched hand.

'Phone first.'

The exchange is made. He takes a couple of steps.

'Don't go any further. How do I know you're not going to make off with my phone?'

Majid decides to text rather than make a call with this crew listening in.

We didn't go north.
Target London.
He looks around.
'Where are we?'
'Are you kidding? You don't know where you are?'
'No, I'm staying at a mate's house.'
'So?'
'He's just moved in. I didn't pay much attention when we were driving.'
He can see the way they're looking at him.
'Come on.'
That's when he sees Bashir's car turning into the street. Bashir stops for a woman to cross.
'Quick!'
'Give me my phone back. You've got your fifteen pounds' worth.'
Majid has dropped behind them to stay out of Bashir's sight. He presses *send*, hands over the phone and hurries back indoors. His heart is slamming. Did Bashir see him? That's when he remembers the snip. He flicks it with his thumb. It makes a loud click. Abu Rashid sits bolt upright in his chair.
'What are you doing over there?' he demands irritably. 'I wish you would sit still.'
Majid drops into his chair. He can barely breathe.
'Sorry.'
The door opens.

Kate flashes her ID and passes through the security cordon. She finds Jack talking to a Special Branch officer.

'We need to talk.'

They find a space overlooking the Convention Centre. Police teams are checking bins, gratings, gutters, anywhere that could conceal an explosive device. Armed officers are setting up positions. A helicopter does a pass overhead.

'I'm surprised you're still here, Kate.'

Kate waves her phone screen at him. 'You've got an event here called Riverside. Just go through the details for me.'

Jack pulls out his iPad and they squat on a wall together.

'It's a Faith Camp. They're holding it at the Riverside Golf Club and Conference Centre.'

He pauses and gives Kate a questioning look.

'Go on,' she says.

Jack scrolls through the information.

'The driving force is an imam called Al Quraishi. We had him under surveillance for a while. He was a trenchant critic of the wars in Iraq and Afghanistan and he has been on the board of a couple of trusts we were interested in. You've read all this Kate, so why do we have to play this game? What have you got?'

'Keep going. Tell me about Al Quraishi.'

Jack looks past her at the skyline of the city.

'He is an opponent of the war on terror and the Prevent strategy. He turned down an invitation to the anti-terrorism conference on the grounds that government policy was alienating young Muslims.'

Kate takes the iPad.

'He is equally critical of the militants, Jack. Have you read these statements? Here we have a credible figure willing to take on the jihadis on their own turf. To somebody like Bashir Mirza, he is an apostate.' Her gaze does not leave him. 'Christian fellowships, Jewish groups, two MPs, a bishop . . . Jack, this is a Who's Who of everything Bashir hates.'

Jack looks put out.

Kate goes on, 'You put this at the bottom of your list? Why?'

'This list didn't amount to much. Tomorrow, Manchester hosts the Home Secretary and most of the security community.'

'And Bashir expects us to be here, drawn to the wrong target. Don't you get it? He has played it perfectly. There were no sightings of his cell north of Newport Pagnell. Nabil has been through the tapes from every service area on the M1 and M6. We're in the wrong place. It's Riverside.'

Jack runs his palm over his nose and mouth.

'You can't be sure it's Riverside. I listed four targets that look more likely.'

Kate runs another search.

'If you had been more thorough, you would have found this photograph. I sent it to your inbox five minutes ago.'

Jack stares at the image and his stomach turns over. It shows Al Quraishi in the company of a younger man.

'Do you recognise him, Jack?'

He nods, dumbstruck.

'It's Bashir Mirza.'

'That's right. Bashir was a member of Al Quraishi's congregation, but Al Quraishi banned him from the mosque for distributing material that promoted hatred. You were so convinced Manchester was the target, you failed to give the other possibilities due attention.'

Jack continues to stare at the photo.

'It's compelling evidence, but where's the proof?'

Kate is about to speak when her phone buzzes. She stares at the screen.

'This is proof.'

She shows him Majid's text.

Target London.

40

Bashir stands in the doorway. He is carrying a large sports bag in his right hand, from which he pulls out a pile of newspapers. He senses the tension between Majid and Abu Rashid.

'What's with you two?'

Abu Rashid turns to the TV.

'There's nothing the matter with me. It's Majid. He's freaking me out.'

Bashir stares at Majid then he crosses the room and pokes Abu Rashid in the chest. Abu Rashid bats his hand away.

'What's your beef, Bashir? I told you, he's the one with the problem.'

Bashir's jaw is set, his eyes hard with anger.

'What are you saying? How's Majid freaking you out?'

Majid's heart is kicking in his chest. He knows what happened to Jamil.

'If you've got any suspicions about Majid, you say it right now, right here. I want to hear it. Has he done anything to jeopardise our operation? Anything?'

Majid watches Abu Rashid's face. *Did he hear the door go? Does he know I was outside?* Both Majid and Abu Rashid's eyes are glittering with fright.

'I got nothing, Bashir. He's just too jumpy, that's all.'

'Well, put up or shut up.'

Bashir flicks Abu Rashid away as if he is an insect.

'You're feeling edgy, Majid, is that right? Have you been watching the news?'

Majid frowns and shakes his head slowly.

'No, why?'

'You're famous.'

Majid pounces on the pile of newspapers, seeing at once the coverage of Amir's arrest and his own departure for Syria.

'What the . . .'

He leafs through them, eyes racing down the columns, stopping at each incriminating photograph.

'How did they get this stuff?' He stares at Bashir. 'We've got to call off the attack.'

Bashir folds his arms.

'The attack goes ahead.'

'They've got my picture.'

'They ain't got Jack. The papers say you're dead. You don't get a better alibi. Say your prayers. Make your preparations. Tomorrow, we take the war to the enemy.'

41

'This isn't living.'

The four of them are sitting in Mum and Dad's room, staring at the TV screen without watching. Amir perches on the bed while his parents take the chairs. Nasima is squatting on the carpet.

'I mean, what are we doing here? This is even worse than the flat.'

'Don't do this, Amir,' Nasima says. 'You know we can't go back. The reporters . . .'

'So we sit and rot in this hotel.'

Mum rests a hand on Amir's arm.

'It is only short term.'

'That's what you said about the flat.'

Glances are exchanged, but nobody speaks, not for some time. The only sound is the roar of traffic outside.

'Well,' Amir says at last, 'is nobody going to say anything?'

Mum stands and places her suitcase on the bed beside Amir. She starts taking clothes out of the wardrobe.

'What are you doing, Ammi-ji?'

Mum turns to her husband.

'There is somewhere we can go, the only place we have ever really felt happy and secure.'

Nasima's heart skips a beat.

'Do you mean it, Mum?'

'Yes, Nasima. I am talking about the house where you and your brothers were born and raised.'

'We're going back to the old house?'

'It is still ours until the estate agent finds a buyer, isn't it? I say we go home.'

Everybody turns and looks at Dad. He nods.

'You're right. We're going home.'

THE PRESENT

42

SATURDAY, 9TH JULY

As Jack guides the hire car past Staples Corner he nudges Kate. She stirs in the passenger seat.

'What time is it? Any news from Riverside?'

'Five o'clock. SCO19 are deployed around the grounds.'

Kate nods. SCO19, the Trojans, the same guys who took out the first cell.

'And the Met has beefed up the police presence?'

'The grounds are crawling with plods. That's the good news.'

Kate inspects herself in the mirror on the back of the car's sunshade. The left side of her face is creased where she has been sleeping with her face against the leather seat. She frowns.

'So give me the bad news.'

'The grounds are extensive. There is parkland to the south and west. Securing the perimeter is an almost impossible task.'

'Why didn't they just cancel the event?'

Jack gives her an apologetic glance.

'Too late. There are coaches coming from other parts of the country. Some of the organisers are there already, staying overnight. They're in a two hundred and thirty-two bed hotel and it's fully booked.'

'I called Nabil,' Jack tells her. 'I don't think he's too happy about being left behind in Manchester. Jen's orders.'

Kate's phone rings. She registers the caller.

'Talk of the devil. Doesn't she ever sleep?'

Jack shakes his head.

'Not when she's got something like this going down.'

'Good morning, Jen. Are you at Riverside?'

'I'm in Manchester. I'm a delegate at the conference.'

Kate grimaces at Jack.

'Of course you are.'

'Keep me in the loop, Kate.'

'That's it?'

'That's it. You called the target correctly. Now finish the job.'

Did Jen just praise me? she wonders.

They stop for a red light. Kate gazes at the rain-damp pavements and the bleary dawn. A few lights are winking in kitchens and living rooms. Jack turns to Kate.

'I think I owe you an apology. I should have listened to you the first time round.'

Kate shrugs.

'We're on the same page now.'

She reaches for the flask of coffee in front of her. It is empty.

'How long now?'

'There is next to no traffic. Forty-five minutes max.'

43

Majid is a few miles away. He wakes and sees the muddy dawn. He looks around the room. Bashir is awake, staring at the ceiling. He doesn't trust anybody. Abu Rashid is snoring noisily. Somehow, Bashir becomes aware of Majid watching him.

'So you're awake, my brother.'

'I'm awake.' He flicks a glance at Abu Rashid. 'I don't know how he sleeps.'

'We're not like him. You see, we think for ourselves. He just takes orders.' Bashir props himself up on his right elbow. 'You think, don't you, Majid?'

Majid can feel the nape of his neck prickling.

'What are you getting at?'

'You've been having doubts. Don't try to deny it.'

Doubts? It is time to brazen it out. No weakness.

'I'm ready.'

Bashir isn't about to be fobbed off.

'That's not what I asked. I'm right, yeah? You've been having doubts?'

Majid wonders how to answer. Any attempt at denial will strike a false note.

'Only a fool thinks he is right all the time. I'm not a fool and neither are you, Bashir. I have doubts. Doesn't mean I'm going to give in to them. You don't need to worry about me.'

Bashir considers this then he holds up a newspaper cutting. It shows Majid's father going into the flat. His blood runs cold.

'What've you got that for?'

'It's insurance.'

'Meaning?'

Bashir spells it out.

'I *do* worry. Yusuf, Jamil, this lump here: they believed everything I said without question. I tell them that ours is a holy jihad and they don't think twice. Our way is the gun. Kill or be killed. We will walk through the gates of Paradise with our heads held high. We're ready because we want to hit back, whatever the price. They accept it all without question. With you, I am never quite sure.'

Majid tells Bashir what he wants to hear.

'Today is for Bosnia, Chechnya, Palestine, Iraq, Afghanistan, Libya, Syria. The enemy's armies entered the Muslim lands so we will strike at the heart of theirs. You can rely on me.'

'That's just it, Majid. I don't hear the same certainty in your voice. Maybe your heart is too soft for war.'

He folds the newspaper article and puts it in his pocket. 'You love your family. That's why I've got this.' His finger lingers over the killer detail. 'I know where they are.' He smiles, lies down and closes his eyes. 'See what I mean? Insurance.'

Bashir could be Omar, ordering death on a rugged hillside. Ten minutes pass, twenty, half an hour, then finally Bashir gets to his feet and kicks Abu Rashid awake.

'Shave your heads. It is time.'

Abu Rashid blows out his cheeks.

'So this is the dawning of the last day of my life.'

Bashir pounds him on the back with the flat of his hand.

'You are a mujahid, my brother. Think of it as the dawning of the first day of your eternal life.'

44

The Sarwar family is home. Last night they slipped into the house under cover of darkness, parking the car two streets away. They used the back way in case the press pack was camped nearby. They weren't ready to explain their return to their neighbours. Now they are having breakfast in their own kitchen.

'It was good to sleep in my own bed,' Nasima says, sipping her apple juice. 'The mattress is so much more comfortable than the one in the flat.'

'Everything in that place was cheap and shoddy,' her father says. 'We would never have ended up in such a place but for Majid.'

Amir speaks without raising his eyes from the table.

'Do you hate him, Abbu-ji?'

There is disbelief in his father's eyes.

'Hate him? I loved him the day he was born. I will love him until the day of my death.' He reaches out and hooks Amir's neck. 'I love you too, Amir.'

'I'm so sorry,' Amir says, his voice thick with emotion. 'I brought all this madness down on our heads.'

It is his mother's turn to reach out to him.

'You did something you believed in. In that, you are your father's son.'

Nasima gets up and walks to the garden window.

'I had almost forgotten how much I love this house.'

Mum joins Nasima and wraps her arms round her.

'I know you do. Your whole life is in these walls. This has always been home.'

'Mum, Dad: can't we stay?'

'What are you saying?'

'We ran away. We left our home and all our friends behind so that we didn't have to face them. We were ashamed of Majid and what he did.' Nasima gathers her thoughts. 'The flat was no safer than this house. Don't you think it's better to look the world in the face instead of running?'

This is the opportunity Amir has been waiting for.

'She's right. What Majid did won't go away just because we pretend it didn't happen. This is where we belong.'

Kate is pacing up and down the main entrance to the Riverside Hotel, waiting for Jen's call. Behind her, the hotel guests are drinking coffee in the open. The staff filled Kate's flask for her. Lifesaver. Some of the residents are watching the police presence with bemusement. The manicured lawns are dotted with tents where various seminars are due to take place. There are placards hammered into the ground. She reads the various signs:

Islam: a religion of peace.
Tolerance or engagement?
Understanding our common ground.
What do we mean by diversity?

Groups of young people are sitting on the grass enjoying the sunshine after the rain. There is a Jewish boy in a kippa engaging a young woman in hijab in earnest conversation. A group of Sikh boys are laughing at something a priest has just said. At the fringes of the event there are armed police officers leaning against their vehicles. They have been told to stay close to their transport so they don't have to display their weapons.

Kate sees Ibrahim Al Quraishi chatting to an Anglican bishop and waving to a passing group of stewards in yellow tabards. She watches all this and imagines a new Utøya. In her mind's eyes, she is a witness to the crackle of gunfire, the screams, the dead and dying. This is the realm she has sworn to defend: families like hers. Innocents. Her phone rings.

'Jen, hi.'

There is the inevitable question.

'It's all quiet here. What about you?'

Jen's voice is calm and measured. 'Nothing to report from the conference. There is something though.'

'Yes?'

'Bedfordshire police have found a body in the woods. It is Jamil Daud.'

'Shot?'

'Stabbed to death. Have you heard from Bungee?'

'No. I think he must have taken a great risk texting me. There is no way Bashir would have let him anywhere near a phone.'

Jen's pinched features are easy to imagine. A dead body. An asset who is out of contact.

'Are you liaising closely with SCO19?'

Kate looks instinctively across the park to where the Trojans' blacked-out Range Rovers are parked.

'We are in permanent contact.'

She doesn't say that the Trojans are keeping her at arm's length.

'Good to hear. Roadblocks?'

'There are roadblocks on all road access to the site.' There is no point burdening Jen with the issues about the perimeter.

'OK, be vigilant.' Then, as an afterthought, Jen adds, 'Stay safe.'

Kate slips her phone into her coat pocket and wanders through the tented village. She looks at the Trojans standing around their Range Rovers. They don't give much away. At best, there is a look of detached boredom.

'Penny for your thoughts.'

It's Jack.

'I'm worried.'

'So what's new? Is this about Bungee?'

'Yes. Jamil Daud just turned up dead. Bungee delivered the intel, but we still don't know where he is.'

Jack is fidgeting. 'I won't be reassured until he delivers Bashir and Abu Rashid. It could still be a trick.'

Kate shakes her head.

'Manchester was the distraction, Jack. This is the target. I know it.'

46

Kate takes a call.

'We've got eyes on a vehicle heading for the service entrance. An A4 team has picked them up on the southern approach road. Black Nissan. Three men inside.'

'Do we have a positive ID?'

'Not yet.'

There is a crackle of radio chatter. Kate approaches the SCO19 officers.

'I'm the MI5 handler. I have an agent in that car.'

'If they get any closer to the gate, we will interdict.'

Kate feels a tug in her stomach.

'The plates belong to a black Escort. It's a stolen vehicle,' an officer tells her.

'You've got to stay back,' Kate insists. 'Give me two minutes.'

She hears a voice spit.

'Spooks.'

Kate meets Jack's gaze.

'I've put a year's work into Majid.'

'Do you really think that's our concern? They are minutes from the gate.'

There is another burst of radio chatter. Kate's blood runs cold.

'Trojan units. We have a positive ID on the occupants.'

The first vehicle pulls away. The second Range Rover starts to roar towards the gate where the third team is waiting. There is a final burst of radio chatter through the open window.

'Trojan units. Attack!'

Kate runs to her car. Jack follows.

'What the hell are you doing?'

'Majid's my agent, Jack. I won't let them kill him.'

'Don't be stupid. Our role is intelligence and surveillance. Leave the action stuff to SCO19.'

'You do what you want, Jack. I'm going.'

47

Abu Rashid is looking over his shoulder.

'What is it?'

'A car in the trees. Back there on a side road.'

Bashir frowns.

'Are you sure?'

Abu Rashid hesitates then nods.

'Yes, I know what I saw.'

Bashir reaches for the magazines.

'Two mags each. This is it.'

They clear the next bend and see the three SCO19 Range Rovers, coming towards them in a line across the road.

'What the hell?'

Bashir's stare is full of hatred.

'Majid.'

All three men move simultaneously. Majid crashes his trainer on to the brake and fights for control of the steering wheel. Abu Rashid is levelling the barrel of his weapon at Majid's head. Majid hits the door handle and throws himself backwards on to the road, firing as he falls. The Range Rovers are approaching, headlights flashing.

'You betrayed us,' Bashir screams, poking his gun through the open door.

Majid kicks the door against the barrel and a burst of

automatic fire rips through the yew trees.

Abu Rashid is yelling with pain. Bashir roars a command.

'Give me covering fire.'

Abu Rashid stumbles out of the car. One arm is incapacitated. It doesn't stop him putting the Škorpion on automatic with his other hand. He sprays the cops with wild fire. The Range Rovers stop in a line. Doors swing open.

'Police! Stand still!'

Abu Rashid is stumbling forward.

'Allahu Akbar!'

'I order you to stop.'

Abu Rashid keeps coming. Three shots cut him off in mid-yell and he falls. Majid scrambles on to the verge. Bashir is executing a three-point turn at high speed, while holding a gun. He is about to fire at Majid when there is another shout.

'Lay down your weapon.'

Then Bashir smiles.

'I know something worse than death, Majid.'

48

Kate brakes and skids to a halt behind the Trojans. She feels a hum of apprehension as they close around her. If that's what she feels like, what is going through Majid's mind right now?

'Stay back,' one of them says. 'We have this under control.'

Kate is fumbling in her coat pocket.

'Stay where you are,' he calls.

In an act of defiance, Kate flashes her ID. Her voice sounds louder than she intends as she struggles to impose some kind of authority.

'I have every right to be here. My agent is over there. He must not be touched. Do you understand?'

The card has little effect, her words even less.

'I want you to step back. Get into the car.'

Kate ducks out of the cop's reach and starts to run. Somebody shouts, but it is her own voice she hears.

'Majid?'

She sees Abu Rashid's body on the carriageway. A stream of blood is running from his head and torso. That's when she spots Majid. He is struggling to his feet. He disarms his weapon and holds up the Škorpion and the magazine.

'I surrender!'

'Police. Put the weapon down.'

It is as if the conversation is taking place in two different dimensions. There is no communication.

'I'm doing it, yeah?'

Kate sees the Trojans approaching. They have their weapons trained on Majid. The whole thing is happening in slow motion.

'Don't shoot,' she yells. 'That man is my asset. I repeat. Do not shoot.'

Her attention is on Majid. Jack has caught up with her. He makes a grab for her sleeve.

'Kate, you're going to get yourself killed.'

She turns and stares.

'What are you saying?'

She feels the throb of fear.

'They're going to kill him, aren't they?'

Majid still has the Škorpion in his right hand and the magazine in his left.

'Majid, drop the weapon. Throw it away. Now!'

She sprints to where the Trojans are approaching Majid. She can see terror in his eyes. He drops to his knees.

'Surrender. I surrender, OK?'

Kate sees that the Glock 17s are still trained on him. She throws herself in front of Majid, arms raised.

'Do not fire.'

She has her ID in her hand. 'This man is my asset.'

'Step away!'

She sees the look in the Trojan's eyes and she imagines the crack of the Glock. That's all it takes, one finger on the trigger, one squeeze, one shot.

'Do not fire.'

The Trojans watch the MI5 officer sheltering her man.

'Do not . . . fire.'

Very slowly, with some deliberation, they lower their weapons. Majid looks around.

'Where's Bashir?'

49

Majid is yelling from the back seat of the car, fingers clawing at his face.

'Can't we go faster? Bashir is after my family.'

Kate turns to look at him.

'You've got to stay calm, Majid.' She has to keep him under some kind of control. 'The police have got the lead now.'

Jack watches Majid's face in the rear-view mirror. His eyes are hostile.

'You're lucky not to be in custody. You were stopped with an automatic weapon half a mile from the Faith Camp. Don't you get that?'

Majid's eyes blaze.

'Don't you get that this man wants to slaughter my family?' He looks around the inside of the vehicle. 'What does it take for you people to understand? This isn't about religion. It isn't even about politics any more. This is revenge, pure and simple.'

There is a storm of fear, anger and bewilderment raging inside Majid. 'At least tell me what's happening. You said a police unit was on its way to the flat.'

'We're dependent on communications from them, Majid. I'll tell you when I know.'

As if in answer to Majid's question, Kate takes a call.

'Yes? OK.'

She turns. There is a troubled look in her eyes.

'What is it? What's wrong?'

'When the police got to the flat, the door had already been kicked in.'

'Is my family OK?'

'They weren't there, Majid. A neighbour said it had been empty for over twenty-four hours. Bashir's gone too.'

'Gone? What do you mean, gone?'

Jack hangs a left.

'We'll be there in five minutes. Maybe we will get a clearer picture then.'

Majid is in panic mode.

'What's the point of going to the flat if he's already moved on?'

Then, realisation:

'Turn the car round!'

'What?'

'Turn the car round. Do it now. I know where he's going.'

Kate looks confused.

'Home. The house where I grew up.'

Jack takes the fourth exit from the roundabout. Majid leans forward, pointing.

'Next right. I'll direct you from here.'

Jack nods.

'Does Bashir know the address?'

'Yes, he has been in my house. He knows everything about me.'

Nasima reads her mother's note.

'Gram flour, fenugreek leaves, potatoes, cauliflower, chilli powder, garam masala . . .' She keeps reading. 'Is that everything?'

'I think so. You've got your phone on you. I'll text you if I remember anything else.'

Nasima pulls a face.

'I'll need extra arms to carry it all.'

'You have extra arms. They are called Amir.'

Amir is too happy to be home to offer a protest. Nasima embraces her mother.

'We won't be long. Are you ready, Amir?'

He zips his jacket.

'Shopping isn't really my thing, but OK.'

Nasima waves the note.

'I hope you're feeling strong.'

They step out of the front door and walk the familiar streets towards the convenience store. It is as if life is starting over. Amir has a question for his sister.

'I like the idea of coming back, for good. Do you think Mum and Dad will go for it?'

Nasima beams.

'Did you see Mum's face this morning? She felt the way we did. She was home.'

'And Dad?'

'She'll win him round, Amir. I know it.'

Amir's gaze roves round the familiar sights. After the events of the last few days it is all so suburban, so ordinary, so safe.

'Tell me the bad times are over.'

Nasima gives him a playful shove.

'We'll be OK. I know it.'

The store is empty so the shopping takes less than five minutes. The twins emerge, deep in conversation. Neither of them notices the silver Ford Focus scream to a halt on the other side of the road. They are about to walk away from the store when Nasima's eyes widen as she glances to her right. Amir follows her gaze and his flesh crawls.

'Bashir!'

'Long time no see, Amir.' He allows the barrel of the Škorpion to drift towards Nasima. 'Now, if you don't want to see your pretty sister's brains on that shop window, I advise both of you to get in the car.'

51

Mum rushes into the living room the moment her husband cries out. She finds him leaning forward, one hand on the back of an armchair, his face taut with shock.

'Naveed?'

There are tears in his eyes. His mouth is moving, but the words don't come out. He hands her the phone, unable to speak.

'Who is this?' she asks, barely daring to put it to her ear.

'Mum, it's me.'

At the sound of his voice, a sob bursts from her, tearing through her chest and filling the room.

'Majid?' Her voice hangs. Then the questions begin. 'How? They told us you were dead.'

She can't believe she is talking to her son.

'There's no time for this. Ammi-ji, the police will be with you in a couple of minutes. Do exactly as they say. Your lives could depend on it.'

Mum's head is spinning.

'The police? Why are the police coming?'

'There's no time to explain. You are in terrible danger. Just get out of there, all of you.'

'Nasima and Amir, they're not here.'

Silence explodes. Then a question.

'Where are they?'

'The Twenty Four Seven next to the library. They went out about five minutes ago.'

Majid thinks.

'Get them on the phone. They've got to sit tight.'

He pauses. 'OK, I'm going to hang up. Call them. Tell them to stay indoors. It is vital they don't move. We're nearly there.'

There is no time to ask who he means by *we*. The street outside is filling with flashing blue lights. Somebody is pounding on the door and shouting their names.

'How many of you are in the house?'

Dad stares in confusion at the scene before him. There is a pair of armed officers with guns resting on their forearms.

'Just the two of us,' he says.

His wife's eyes have just registered panic.

'Naveed. They're not answering.'

52

Majid sees the silver Focus the moment they pass the library.

'That's him!'

He has the door open before Jack has even stopped the car. He stumbles, but he manages to hit the ground running, trainers pounding along the pavement. He registers everything in slow motion: Nasima and Amir facing Bashir, the open car door, the gun. A shopper is beginning to scream. Her voice makes Amir turn. 'Majid?'

Alerted to Majid's approach, Bashir struggles out of the vehicle, using his thumb to set the Škorpion to automatic. In that split-second, Amir knows that his brother's life is in danger. He hurls himself at the gunman, sending him crashing against the car door. A burst of fire chatters into the sky. Pedestrians scream and run for cover.

Bashir pushes Amir back, trying to aim the Škorpion at his chest. Nasima does the only thing she can, swinging the shopping bag in her right hand with all her might. It connects with the barrel just as Bashir squeezes the trigger. A second burst of fire takes out two windows above the shops and sends hot metal ricocheting off walls. A SCO19 Range Rover has mounted the pavement and officers are spilling out. Majid races towards Bashir. The Trojans have fanned out, ready to fire.

'Stop! Police!'

In the confusion, they don't have a clear shot. Before Bashir can aim or fire, Majid crashes his foot into the car door. Bashir is trapped, his arm limp. Majid wrenches the door open and smashes his fist into Bashir's face. Blood sprays across his skin. The Trojans are close enough to take a shot.

There is a command directed at Majid.

'Step back.'

'Stand still. Do not move.'

Majid is not moving away. He can hear the Trojans shouting. He shakes his head. This is his chance. He slams Bashir's hand on the top of the door, making him cry out as a bone snaps. He repeats the action and the Škorpion falls to the pavement.

'You're a traitor, Majid. Apostate! Enemy of Islam.'

Majid laughs in his face.

'You're a fraud. You ruined my life . . . for nothing. For you.'

Bashir spits in Majid's face.

'I will see you in Hell.'

The police lead the struggling Bashir away. Kate approaches the agent she has nurtured so carefully. Majid embraces his brother and sister.

Nasima is sobbing. It is Amir who finds the words.

'What are you doing here? You're supposed to be dead.'

'So everybody keeps saying.'

Majid wraps an arm round Amir's head the way he always did.

'We'll talk later. Let's get you home.'

THE PRESENT

SUNDAY, 10TH JULY

Kate has been expecting Jen's call. It should be routine, informing her that the Manchester conference has gone off without any problems. She knows by the tone of her voice that she isn't going to get any recognition for her efforts. She called the target correctly, but nobody is handing out brownie points.

'What's wrong?'

Jen clears her throat. Kate recognises it as a gesture of irritation.

'I have just had the Commissioner on the phone, Kate.'

The Commissioner of the Metropolitan Police.

'He is very unhappy about Five's role in what happened at Riverside.'

Kate leaps to the service's defence.

'It is because of our information that the Met was able to avert a massacre. But for our intel, they would have been unprepared for the attack.'

Jen doesn't even respond.

'You interfered with SCO19's operational decisions, Kate. You drove your car into the line of fire and put yourself and those police officers at risk.'

Kate realises that this is serious.

'I was stopping them shooting my agent.'

'*Our* agent.' Jen's tone is even and considered. 'You put

yourself in the line of fire, Kate. You insisted on taking Majid with you, even though he was emotionally involved.'

'Majid reacted with great courage. He saved lives.'

'SCO19 officers were on the scene. They had the lead.'

'It was Majid who saved his family, not the police.'

'You will be transferred to other duties, Kate, with immediate effect. You got too close to your agent. It compromised your judgement. Firearms were discharged twice on the streets of London.'

'Jen, I know I took risks, but Majid came through for us. He helped us identify the target. He saved lives.'

Jen's tone remains neutral.

'Kate, Nabil is in charge of our asset from hereon in. You will return to Millbank immediately. That is an order.'

Kate closes her eyes as she answers.

'I'm on my way.'

54

Majid listens to the sound of cooking in the kitchen. Nasima is sitting next to him on the settee, while Amir lolls in the armchair opposite, playing with his phone. Nasima leans against him, as if reassuring herself that he is back. He watches the alien normality of the house through a thin, translucent membrane of memory. A glance to his right takes him to the table where he taught Amir to arm wrestle. A glance to the left reminds him of wiping Nasima's tears after she took a tumble.

Then the walls spill recollections of his own fall, his descent into hell. There are the endless quarrels with his father, his slow detachment from his family, the influence of Bashir. Majid is home, but he is in a bubble. His thoughts are still on that Syrian hillside. Omar's voice breaks through the hum of domesticity.

'*You know what to do?*'

Majid has his weapon trained on the three kneeling men. What was disillusion has become despair. He is one squeeze of a trigger from self-hatred. He has told himself over and over again that he came to heal.

Yusuf boasted of the destruction he was going to visit on his enemies. Am I really much better? Majid wonders, as the gun weighs heavy in his hands, pregnant with death.

'Is there a problem?'

Yes, *Majid tells himself,* there is a problem, Omar, and it is you. You and every murderer like you.

He knows what to do.

THE PAST

SUMMER, 2014

'Is there a problem?'

Majid could hardly breathe. The muzzle of his rifle was pressing against the back of his captive's head. He could feel the rhythm of the man's breathing through the stock. This slight pressure, this little bit of resistance, it was life; and this finger on the trigger, his finger, was death.

'No problem.'

He met Omar's gaze. He had come to hate those cold, implacable eyes. Not once in all these months had Majid felt it as clearly as this, his utter revulsion for everything this man and all the butchers like him stood for. He had come to help the victims of war. At least, that's what he had told himself. He stared at the weapon he was holding as if seeing it for the first time. He wasn't protecting anyone. He was just one more killer with a gun. A word escaped his lips.

'Home.'

Omar frowned.

'What did you say?'

Majid stared dumbly into Omar's face.

Home.

I want to go home.

Majid stared into Omar's thoughts. What are you waiting for? *You've had your orders. Do it. Kill them.* Suddenly, Majid's mind was clear. He would not slay his unarmed brothers. He would kill the monster who craved martyrdom.

Majid gripped his weapon firmly and turned the muzzle on Omar. He was aware of the muscles in Omar's face slackening. Yes, even cold-blooded killers feel that moment of despair as they look death in the eye. Majid was aware of Yusuf reacting somewhere to his left, but he had the drop on them all. Omar was a dead man.

Then something flickered into view, a silvery object, bright and somehow beautiful against the cloudless sky. A MiG-29 was about to attack. Before he could squeeze the trigger, Majid felt himself being lifted off his feet. He was a ghost, weightless, flimsy as a child's toy. Something hit him like a baseball bat and pain ripped through his chest and neck. When the first shockwave ebbed, leaving him lying in a pool of agony, Majid looked up.

They were all dead. Every one of them. Yet he lived. God had spared him.

Feeling returned to Majid's legs and he staggered painfully to his feet. He could have lain down in the hot sun and succumbed to his wounds. He could have surrendered to the dark. Instead, he started to stumble forward, hugging his ribs.

The Turkish border was just a few miles over the next hill and beyond that lay home.

THE PRESENT

MONDAY, 11TH JULY

'Penny for them?'

Majid glances at Nasima. She is smiling.

'A penny for your thoughts. You were miles away.'

Majid squeezes her hand.

'It's been one hell of a journey.' He smiles. 'But I'm home now. You can't imagine how many times I thought about phoning and telling you I was alive.' He crushes his palms together, trying to squeeze the last year into dust. 'I am never going away again.'

His father comes in from the kitchen. He rests a hand on Majid's shoulder.

'We will help you rebuild your life,' he says. 'As a first step, we will make this our family's home once more.'

Nasima leaps up and wraps her arms round her father's neck.

'You mean it?'

'We mean it.'

Amir is sitting up.

'That's brilliant, Dad.'

Majid is about to add something when he notices a car pull up outside. Mum answers the knock at the door. Majid recognises the newcomers. One of them is Jack, the other . . .

'You!'

It is Nabil.

'That's right, Majid, your friend from the train. My job was to carry out surveillance.'

'What are you doing here?'

Nabil looks around.

'Is there somewhere we can talk privately?'

Majid doesn't budge.

'I won't have any more secrets from my family.'

Nabil makes a decision. He nods to Jack and his colleague leaves the room. 'You're my agent now, Majid.'

'Agent?' Majid watches Jack leave the room. 'I did everything you people asked. That was the deal. I give you Bashir. You give me my freedom. No prison sentence. I get to go home.'

Amir knows something is wrong.

'What's going on? Why are you here?'

Amir's words focus Majid.

'That's what I want to know. Where's Kate? I want to see her.'

Nabil sits down and crosses his legs.

'Any verbal agreement you think you had—'

'Think?' Majid clenches his fists. 'What do you mean, *think*? Nabil, I know what she said. She promised me my freedom in exchange for Bashir. I kept my side of the bargain.'

He gets up and crosses the room, shouting into the front garden, 'Kate?'

There are footsteps, but it is Jack.

'What's happened to Kate?' Majid demands. 'I have to see her.'

'She's gone.'

'Where? Call her. Tell her to come back. I am not saying another word until she is in this room.' He folds his arms. 'OK, you need to explain what this is all about.'

Nabil is unperturbed by Majid's agitation.

'You are our asset, Majid. We have another job for you.'

Majid is shaking his head.

'No. No way. I did everything that was asked of me. This is over. You don't get anything more from me.'

'One more job, Majid. We don't have an asset as credible as you.'

Mum joins the rest of the family. She glares at Nabil.

'How can you ask any more of him? He could have been killed. Why can't you leave us alone?'

'I'm no use to you,' Majid says. 'Bashir knows I'm alive. My cover is blown.'

'Bashir Mirza boasted about his contacts. We are pretty sure it was all bombast. We will give you a new identity. There is more mileage in Bungee yet. We are fighting a war. We need soldiers like you.'

Majid's heart is hammering.

'Soldiers? That's what Omar called me. I'm done being a soldier. Don't you get it? I just want my life back.'

Nabil glances at his phone.

'You could still be looking at a ten-to-twelve year prison sentence for your time in Syria. If you do this for us, I am sure we can clear that for you.'

Amir is staring at Nabil with eyes that are dark with rage.

'But for my brother there would be hundreds of people dead. Doesn't that count for anything? You can't do this to him.'

'It is Majid's choice,' Nabil drawls. 'All I have done is remind him of the consequences of refusal.'

'Prison.'

'Almost certainly, yes.'

Majid is silent. Finally, he looks up.

'I don't have any choice. One last job.'

'One last job,' Nabil confirms.

Mum is in tears.

'Can't we at least have a few days with our son? All this time we thought he was dead. Just when we got him back . . . It's so cruel.'

Nabil considers her words.

'We have to preserve Majid's anonymity at all costs. If a single reporter got a photo of him the way he looks now, there could be no deal.'

'He would go to prison?'

'Yes.' Nabil walks to the door. 'You have five minutes to come to a decision. I'll be waiting in the car.'

Majid embraces his mother and father.

'I'm so sorry, Ammi-ji, Abbu-ji. I thought it was all over. I've got to do this.'

'No!'

'I'll come back to you, I promise. Trust me.'

Nasima buries her face in his shoulder.

'It's so unfair.'

Majid pulls Amir to him.

'You be good, yeah? Study hard. Make a life for yourself. You and Nasima, you do something I never did and make our parents proud.'

Dad wraps his hand round the back of Majid's neck and pulls him close.

'My son, I could not be prouder of you than I am at this moment.' His eyes glisten with tears. 'You *will* come home. Insha'Allah.'

Majid gives each member of his family a last embrace then walks to the door.

'I will be back, I promise. I love every one of you. God willing, I will return and life will be good again.'

There are further murmurs of *Insha'Allah*.

Then he is gone.